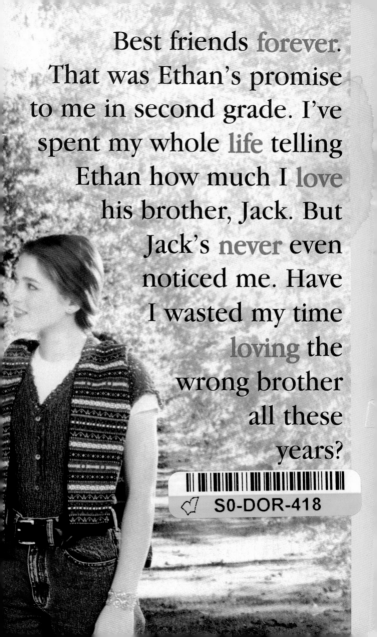

Best friends forever. That was Ethan's promise to me in second grade. I've spent my whole life telling Ethan how much I love his brother, Jack. But Jack's never even noticed me. Have I wasted my time loving the wrong brother all these years?

S0-DOR-418

# Brotherly love . . .

"You're so beautiful," Jack murmured in my ear.

Jack was saying exactly what I wanted him to say. What I had dreamed he would say. And I was finally in his arms, dancing with him under the moonlight.

I looked up into Jack's green eyes and felt my knees go weak. He tilted my chin up and leaned down. I smelled his minty breath just before his lips touched mine.

But suddenly the terrace was bathed in bright light.

"Oops! Sorry." It was Ethan. "I heard voices out here, and I came to check things out. Sorry if I interrupted," Ethan said. He seemed to be ignoring Jack's hostile glare. "Hi, Gigi."

"Hi, Ethan."

Jack wrapped his arms around me again. But somehow the bright lights and Ethan's sudden appearance had changed my mood. A moment ago Jack was about to kiss me. I had waited an eternity for that moment, and I could tell that Jack was ready to pick up where he had left off—with Ethan standing right there.

But I was embarrassed that Ethan had caught us. All I knew was that I had to get out of there. As much as I'd wanted to kiss Jack—to have Jack kiss me—I didn't feel like having any witnesses, especially not Ethan.

"I—I have to go now," I stammered, shrugging out of Jack's grasp. Then I turned and ran home.

Don't miss any of the books in *Love Stories*
—a romantic new series from Bantam Books!

Love Stories

# Love Changes Everything

## ARLYNN PRESSER

BANTAM BOOKS
NEW YORK · TORONTO · LONDON · SYDNEY · AUCKLAND

RL 6, age 12 and up

LOVE CHANGES EVERYTHING
*A Bantam Book / October 1995*

*Produced by Daniel Weiss Associates, Inc.*
*33 West 17th Street*
*New York, NY 10011*

ISBN: 0-553-56665-2

*Published simultaneously in the United States and Canada*

Bantam Books are published by Bantam Books, a division of Bantam
Doubleday Dell Publishing Group, Inc. Its trademark, consisting of the
words "Bantam Books" and the portrayal of a rooster, is Registered in
U.S. Patent and Trademark Office and in other countries. Marca
Registrada. Bantam Books, 1540 Broadway, New York, New York 10036.

PRINTED IN THE UNITED STATES OF AMERICA

OPM    0 9 8 7 6 5 4 3 2 1

# Chapter One

Dear Becky,

I still can't believe I'm actually, finally on my way to Paris. When Dad dropped me off at the airport this morning it was still dark, and I was so sleepy I wasn't even thinking.

Actually I was trying not to think about you-know-who. Jack.

Last night he invited Lydia Joyner over for a private party. Just the two of them. I saw them lounging on the pool terrace from my bedroom window. They were even sharing a lounge chair—as if the Chandlers don't

1

have enough! They must have been practicing conservation of lounge chairs.

Lydia, with her perfect model face, her perfect long blond hair cascading down to her hips—you know how she is. Her dress was so tight it was almost indecent. I was so mad—after all, it was my last night in Winnetka for an entire year. Silly me. I had thought maybe, just maybe, Jack would have invited me over for an intimate farewell party.

Right—dream on, Gerolyn. As if I could compete with Lydia Joyner.

When Jack and Lydia started kissing, I slammed my window shut and pulled down the shade. I'd seen enough.

I tried to do what you suggested. I wrote out a list of Jack's bad qualities, but I couldn't think of any—except his interest in Lydia, that is. So instead I started writing everything I loved about him. I wrote four full pages!

I would have written more, but my pen ran out of ink. I put the list in an envelope with a newspaper photo of him in his football uniform.

Actually, I almost did stop by the Chandlers' last night. I ran into Ethan as he was going out for a run and I was coming in from some last-minute shopping—I heard a nasty rumor that you can't get decent peanut butter in France, so I had to stock up. Ethan asked me to stop by later, after I finished packing, and say good-bye.

I had planned to go over till I saw that Lydia was already there. No point in stopping by just to see Ethan. I saw him in class all last semester, and this summer we kept bumping into each other at the lake or on the bike paths. He knows I have a major crush on his older brother, and I think it makes him uncomfortable—you know, the whole dating thing.

I don't think Ethan's ever even been on a date. Do you? He spends all his time running and studying. Jack and Ethan are so different. It's hard to believe they're even brothers, much less only a year apart.

Enough about me and my pathetic, nonexistent love life. I'm off to Paris! Write soon. I miss you already.

Love,
Gerolyn

*Dear Becky,*

*Bonjour! I'm sitting in a café, sipping a café au lait and watching these incredibly cute French college students. They all smoke, which I think is gross, but they look so intense hunched over their coffees, talking to each other as if they're solving the world's problems. I can understand a word or two of what they say, but they speak so much faster than we speak in class. It's like a totally different language.*

*My host family, the Thibaults, are really nice. They make me feel completely at home. I've got my own room and my own bathroom. It's so great.*

*Most of my classes are given in French—math, science, etc.—and I have special French-language classes to help me keep up. I also have a tutor to help me with my homework. She's great! Her name is Véronique and she's eighteen. Even though she's only a few years older than we are, she's so sophisticated! You wouldn't believe what she wears to school—she looks like she's* going on a fashion shoot instead of to the lycée (that's what they call high school here).

I'm going shopping with Véronique this weekend. She said it would be a good learning experience for me to have more contact with French culture—and to practice my conversation skills. We're going to Printemps, one of the big Parisian department stores, then we're off to some of her favorite boutiques. I can't wait!

What's happening at home? Have you seen Jack at school? Is he dating anyone? I guess, being a junior, he wouldn't have time for sophomore girls like us—except, of course, Lydia Joyner. Don't spare any of the gory details.

Love,
Gerolyn


September 21
Versailles


Dear Becky,

We're here in Versailles, which is about twelve miles from Paris, on a class trip. We visited a chateau (that's a palace) built by a king of France over three hundred years ago. It's huge—even bigger than the Chandler mansion. There's a hallway that has windows along one of the long sides and mirrors along the other. The roof is curved like an arch all the way down, and there are paintings on the ceiling. It's incredibly beautiful.

Since I've been in France, I've seen so many exquisite buildings and stained glass and stuff like that, but this blows everything away. After we walked through the palace, my class sat in the gardens and ate a picnic lunch. I was thinking about how before I came to France, I couldn't imagine a house bigger or more beautiful than the Chandlers' mansion. But their entire house would look smaller than my carriage house compared to Versailles.

Oops, the bus is loading. I've got to go.

Love,
Gerolyn

September 30
The cafeteria at the
International School

Dear Becky,
I finished eating already and have

some time before my next class, and I couldn't wait till tonight to tell you what I did.

I've decided that it's time for me to get over Jack Chandler once and for all. I can't keep carrying around this crush—it's, like, crushing me! (Okay, bad pun.)

I think living in the carriage house behind his mansion only made it worse. At times I felt like I knew Jack so well from watching him all those years. I had hundreds of conversations with him in my mind. I'd even dream about him. But whenever we were actually in the same place at the same time, it was as if I were invisible.

I knew if I continued reading the list of positives I had written about Jack and staring at his picture every night before I went to bed, like I've been doing since I got here, I wouldn't stop loving him. So—I know you won't believe this—last night I ripped up the list and the photo and even the envelope I had kept them in and threw the whole thing into the trash.

But when I went to bed, I couldn't help dreaming about him. I was swimming with him in the Chandlers' pool.

Jack was wearing red lifeguard trunks, and I was wearing a slinky black swimsuit (like something Lydia Joyner would wear).

We were playing tag and splashing and having fun. Then I realized that I could breathe underwater like a mermaid, and so could Jack. We stayed underwater, and then he kissed me—while we were still underwater.

Then I woke up.

Becky, what do you think it means? Am I losing my mind?

When I woke up, I picked up the bits of his photograph and taped them back together. I just stuffed the list of his qualities into another envelope. I already knew them by heart.

I miss you.

Grosses bises,
Gerolyn
October 20
Paris

Dear Becky,

I have a new name—Gigi. No one in France can pronounce my name, and I got tired of having to spell it over and over, so Véronique suggested I take a French name.

*What do you think?*

*I love it and I plan to keep it even when I get back to Winnetka. I feel like a different person here in Paris. It's only right that I have a new name, too!*

*Write soon.*

*Love,*
*Gigi*
*October 29*
*Chez les Thibaults*

Dear Dad,

I'm sitting in my room at the Thibaults', taking a break from studying. Madame Thibault made this incredible meal for us tonight—roast chicken, vegetables, rice, salad, and an apple tart for dessert. I know it doesn't sound so incredible, but everything tastes better in France—no offense to your cooking, Dad. I think it's the way they use spices, or maybe the ingredients are just fresher.

Sometimes I go to the market with Madame Thibault. She doesn't shop in a supermarket like we have at home. There are dozens of stalls with different fruits and vegetables. Several stalls have only cheeses. Some of the cheeses are pretty stinky, but most of them are delicious.

Madame Thibault also goes to the bakery every day for fresh bread. I love it! It's so crusty on the outside and fluffy on the inside.

But it's not just the food that's different here, or the language. It's everything! I'm so happy you let me come. I know it wasn't easy saving the money for this year abroad—I really appreciate it. I feel like I'm changing more and more every day, and not just because I'm learning French. Part of it is living with the Thibaults, especially Madame Thibault. She's so nice—she calls herself my *maman française*, my French mom. I never realized how much I missed having a mother till I came here. Not that you didn't do a great job raising me by yourself after Mom died. But being here in France now, I feel like I'm finally getting a chance to grow up.

I guess this is my roundabout way of saying thank you.

I love you, Daddy,<br>Gerolyn

P.S. Have you seen Jack Chandler around? What's he up to these days? Tell him I said hi.

*Dearest Gerolyn,*

It's lonely here on Christmas morning without you. But the Chandlers took pity on this poor, lonely widower and invited me to Christmas dinner. They always have a wonderful spread, and I'm sure this meal will last me till New Year's.

I remember years ago, I felt awkward as a guest at their house, since my parents used to work for Mr. Chandler's parents. But they've always treated me like a neighbor, not like the son of their former chauffeur and cook. And when your mother died, and you were just a small child, they were especially kind, renting the carriage house to us for almost nothing and having the boys' nanny look after you as well. If it hadn't been for them, I don't think I could have finished law school. I don't know why I'm thinking so much about the past these days—it must be because it's the holidays, a time for reminiscing.

I love getting your letters and hearing about your adventures in France.

11

The bike trip to the Loire Valley sounded fantastic. I tacked the postcards of the chateaux on the bulletin board over my computer. It's hard to believe that people actually lived in those huge stone castles hundreds of years ago. I'm glad you've gotten a chance to see them.

Mrs. Chandler always asks about you. She sends her love, as do the rest of the Chandlers. We all miss you, especially at Christmas.

Love,
Dad


New Year's Day
Paris


Dear Becky,

I had the most fabulous New Year's Eve. My tutor, Véronique, set me up on a real date! Her aunt and uncle and their family are in Paris for the holidays, and Véronique's cousin Philippe is just a year older than we are—and gorgeous! He took me out to dinner at a cute little bistro, then we rode to the top of the Eiffel Tower and watched the fireworks. It was fantastic!

*Philippe even kissed me at midnight. I'd never kissed a guy who smoked before. The weird thing was that even though it was all so romantic, I didn't feel myself falling for Philippe. I think he felt the same way. But we're definitely friends, and he's invited me to visit him where he lives in Provence— that's in the southern part of France.*

*I wish you could come and visit. You would love it here.*

*Love,*
*Gigi*

*P.S. Did you go to any New Year's parties? Who else was there? Anyone with the initials J.C.?*

*March 21*
*Paris*

*Dear Becky,*

*Last Saturday night I went out with one of the boys from my French lit class. He took me to Disneyland Paris, and we had a blast. Bernard doesn't speak any English, but my French is good enough for us to communicate pretty well. Bernard reminds me a little* of Jack. He put his arm around me on one of the scarier rides, and I tried to imagine he was Jack. But it didn't work. Not that I was totally surprised. I mean, if it was that easy for me to find a substitute for Jack, I couldn't really be in love with him, right?

We have vacation next week, and I'm going to visit Philippe in Provence. I wish you could come with me. I miss having my best friend to talk to. Write soon.

Love,
Gigi

April 10
Paris

Dear Becky,

Wow! The south of France was breathtaking. There are all these old villages with stone houses that look like they were built in the Middle Ages (actually some of them were!). And the food! Philippe's mom, Madame Pujolas, is an even better cook than Madame Thibault—which is saying a lot!

The weird thing is that even though

I feel like I'm always eating, I've actually lost a few pounds. I think it's because they eat less meat and smaller portions here and no one snacks between meals. Everyone talks during dinner and we eat slowly, enjoying every mouthful.

I got back to Paris last week and I felt like I was coming home. When I grow up, I think I want to live in Paris. It's so cosmopolitan. Besides, I can't become a famous journalist living in Winnetka, Illinois, all my life. There isn't enough news there to write about.

Now for the biggest news of all (I saved it for last)—I got my hair highlighted! Véronique took me to the place where she gets her hair done. I was so scared. When the colorist was finished, I was afraid to look at myself in the mirror. You know how my hair was always that mousy brown color? Well, it's still brown, but it's got some golden strands now. It really brightens me up, I think. And not only did I change my hair color, I changed my ears! Véronique said they were cute, and she persuaded me to get them pierced—which I did! I love the little gold studs I'm wearing now. In a couple of weeks, I can wear any earrings I want. Véronique already gave me a pair of elegant gold hoops. I can't wait to try them on. She says that I look très élégante (that's very elegant).

Véronique also gave me a makeover to go with my new hair color, and she went with me to buy tons of new cosmetics. She said I had all the wrong colors in my makeup kit—and she was right. I also think I was wearing too much eye makeup, and my lip gloss was too shiny. The next day at school, some of the boys were doing double takes as I walked past them. Bernard asked me out again, but I turned him down. He reminds me too much of Jack, and I'm trying so hard to stop thinking about him.

I sent Jack a postcard, and he never even wrote back. I wonder if he ever got it. Do you think you could ask him next time you see him? Try to make it casual—like, "So, have you heard from Gerolyn?"

Write soon.

Love,
Gigi

*Dear Becky,*

*You know how I keep trying to get over Jack? Well, I was talking about him with Véronique (she calls him Jacques— I love the way that sounds!), and she didn't understand why I was trying to forget about him.*

*"Why not just go after him?" she suggested.*

*I tried to explain that Jack was going to be a senior and I was only going to be a junior. That he was, like, the richest, most popular guy at Winnetka High, and I was, well, not the richest or the most beautiful girl.*

*She said the secret was to act more mysterious, more alluring. She showed me how to turn my head to look at a boy and how to give him a mysterious smile—sort of a half smile. She said no man could resist that smile. I practiced my mysterious smile all day at school, and she was right! Two boys asked me out before the day was over!*

*I have finals next week, then school is over. And here's the best news: Dad said I could stay with the Thibaults all sum-*

17

mer. They're going to Greece in August and taking me with them! I'm so excited. I know you and I were planning to do stuff together this summer, but I couldn't pass up this opportunity. I don't know when I'll ever get the chance to come back to Europe or go to Greece. I hope you're not mad at me.

Love,
Gigi

July 20
Auvergne

Dear Becky,

Last weekend a few of us from school went on a field trip to le Centre—that's what they call the middle area of France. We rode a bus up to the top of Le Puy-de-Dôme, which is a huge extinct volcano. I could see for miles all around us. There are lots of extinct volcanoes and lakes nearby. From the observation area, the volcanoes looked like mountains of green ice cream with a huge scoop taken out of the top.

Of course, that made me think of the Depot and how much I miss their double-thick milk shakes. I don't think you can get a decent milk shake in all of France.

The countryside here is so different from anything I've ever seen. I guess there are volcanoes in the United States; I've just never seen any. There certainly aren't any near Winnetka. Being in such a different place makes me feel different, too. I wonder—if I stayed in France for the rest of my life, would I always miss getting ice cream at the Depot, or would I eventually forget all about everything in Winnetka? (Except you!)

Sometimes I feel so lonely. I know that sounds strange, especially after I just wrote about going away with a bunch of friends here. But I miss being able to look out my bedroom window down onto the Chandlers' pool, watching Jack swim laps. He cuts through the water like a motorboat, leaving a wake behind him. (Okay, so I'm exaggerating a little.)

Then other times I don't think I want to go home at all. I feel like I've learned so much this past year—about life, about myself—and I'm afraid that when I come home, I'll leave all that behind at the Paris airport.

I'm glad you like my new name. Dad refuses to use it when he writes to me. I remind him in every letter I send him, but it's no use.

*This afternoon I'm going to* la piscine *(that's the pool). Everyone here is really into swimming, and there are lots of pools in Paris.*

*What's happening in Winnetka this summer? Did the Chandlers go to their summer country house as usual? Anyone pool-hopping in the Chandlers' pool while they're gone? Fill me in on all the news.*

*Love,*
*Gigi*

*August 9*
*Mykonos*

*Dear Becky,*

*The Greek islands are heaven! We arrived in Athens last week and spent a couple of days sightseeing there. It was fascinating, but the city is so smoggy it's hard to breathe. And all that pollution is eating away at the ruins. It's so sad!*

*The past few days we've been island-hopping, taking a ferry from one island to another. Sometimes we spend the day at the beach. Other times we explore the old ruins. I bought a book on Greek mythology. It's so cool to read about a place when you're actually there. I wish you were here. You'd love it—everything except the food. Too much olive oil! Yech!*

*I'll be home a few days before school starts—I can't believe we're going to be juniors! I've missed you so much. I can't wait to show you all the clothes I've bought. They're not like anything you can find in Winnetka. And with my new hair and new look, I know Jack won't be able to resist me.*

*Love,*
*Gigi*

**August 20**

*Dearest Gerolyn,*

*I wanted to make your homecoming a special day, but unfortunately I have to go away on business. I'm flying out just a few hours after you arrive on Friday. I asked Mrs. Chandler if Jack or Ethan could drive me to the airport, then pick you up and take you home. She assured me it would be no problem. Funny, having one of the Chandlers chauffeur us around—what a switch!*

*I'll only be gone overnight, so we'll have most of the weekend together* before you start school on Monday.

I hope Winnetka won't be too dull after your year abroad. I rented some Julia Child videotapes and have almost perfected my béarnaise sauce. I'm so glad you're coming home.

Love,
Dad

August 22
Paris

Dear Becky,

I can't believe my year abroad is almost over. I keep worrying that when I get back to Winnetka, Gigi will disappear and I'll turn back into plain old Gerolyn—that awkward, unsure fifteen-year-old girl who follows Jack Chandler around like a puppy dog.

I can't wait to see you! The Thibaults gave me a farewell dinner, and everyone knew exactly what to give me as good-bye gifts—clothes, earrings, and more clothes. I'll be the best-dressed junior in Winnetka High history!

See you soon!

Love,
Gigi

# Chapter Two

AS I WALKED off the plane in Winnetka, Illinois, I fought to calm my racing heart. I couldn't wait to see Jack—for him to see me. The new me, Gigi.

I passed through customs like a zombie, claimed my suitcases, and joined the crowd at the gate that led to the terminal.

I looked at the mass of faces around me. Where was Jack? Dad's letter hadn't said for sure that Jack would be there to meet me, but I had wished for it so hard on the plane coming over that I'd convinced myself it would happen just as it had in my daydreams.

Of course, Jack would be looking for the same old ponytailed Gerolyn. When he saw me, he'd do a double take, or maybe he wouldn't even recognize me at all.

23

Then when Jack finally realized who I was, he'd be struck speechless. I would give him my mysterious smile, and he'd become mine forever. . . .

My eyes continued to scan the crowd. He had to be there somewhere. He just had to be.

Suddenly I heard a familiar male voice shout "Gerolyn!" at the top of his lungs.

Dad!

He grabbed me in a tight bear hug and squeezed me till I could hardly breathe. I felt my eyes start to tear up. I knew he had missed me a lot, but I hadn't realized how much I had missed him till just that moment.

"Don't you remember, Dad?" I said when I could breathe again. "I'm Gigi now. Not Gerolyn."

"Whatever you say, sweetheart," he said in a rush. "Look at you! You look beautiful." He clasped my hand. "Listen, I'm sorry, sweetheart, but I've got to run. My plane is boarding now. I'm glad I got to see you. When I found out your flight was delayed, I was afraid I'd miss you altogether."

"Where's Jack?" I asked. "I thought he was coming with you."

"He was busy. Ethan came instead," Dad said.

That's when I noticed Ethan standing right behind him. I tried to hide my disappointment that he was there instead of his brother.

"Gotta go," my dad said. "Love you." He picked up his briefcase and overnight bag, gave me another bone-crushing hug, and ran off toward his gate.

Ethan was just staring at me—he hadn't said a word. But I didn't take it personally. I knew Ethan wasn't the talkative type. He never had been. Even when we were little kids and played together, he rarely spoke more than a few words to me. It didn't bother me—it was just the way he was.

"Hey, Ethan," I said. "Thanks for coming to get me."

"No problem." He picked up my suitcases, and we headed toward the exit and out to the parking lot. Ethan walked a few steps ahead of me, cutting a path through the crowded airport.

"How's Jack?" I asked his back.

"The same," Ethan answered. "He's at football practice. He'll be the starting quarterback this year."

"But school hasn't even begun," I pointed out.

"A lot of the varsity teams had tryouts and practices already."

Although my mind was on Jack and how he'd react to the new me, I couldn't help noticing that Ethan had done some changing himself during the past year.

He was taller than I remembered, and he walked through the crowd with an air of confidence. It wasn't so long ago that he'd been a scrawny, nerdy kid who depended on his big brother to protect him from the class bullies.

I had two huge suitcases filled with new clothes and makeup and souvenirs. I knew they weighed a ton, but Ethan carried them as if they were empty. He must have been lifting weights, I thought, and I studied his biceps as they bulged from beneath his T-shirt. He wasn't as muscular as Jack—not by a long shot—but no one would describe him as scrawny, either.

Ethan tossed the bags into the back of his black Jeep. It was a good thing he hadn't taken his mother's red Miata—the bags would never have fit.

When we were finally on our way out of the airport, Ethan said, "I almost didn't recognize you."

"It's my hair," I said.

"No," Ethan said. "Not just the hair."

"The earrings?" I asked, fingering the gold hoop in my left ear.

He shook his head, glancing at me as often as he could while driving.

"My clothes?" I volunteered. Before my year abroad, I'd worn mostly baggy jeans and T-shirts. Now I had on a patterned bodysuit with snug black leggings. I had spent hours deciding on this outfit. For Jack . . .

"No, it's not that, either," Ethan said, his eyes widening. "It's really strange. You seem so different, so . . ."

I turned and gave him my mysterious smile. I had to practice to make sure I got it just right for Jack. A horn honked, reminding Ethan that the light had turned green.

"Where to now?" I asked, adjusting my seat belt.

"Don't you want to go home?" Ethan asked.

If Jack had been at the house, I'd have made a beeline for home. But with Dad away and Jack at football practice, getting back to our little carriage house behind the Chandlers' palatial mansion was the last thing I wanted to do.

"Can we go somewhere else?" I asked.

"Sure. Anywhere you want to go," Ethan said with a shrug. "What did you miss the most while you were gone?"

"The Depot," I said without hesitation. "I can really go for a double chocolate chip milk shake."

"You know the Depot takes forever," Ethan warned.

"The service hasn't gotten any better?"

He shook his head. "Nope. It's all part of the atmosphere. If they changed, we wouldn't recognize the Depot."

"I don't want you to waste your entire afternoon with me . . . if, you know, it's going to take forever."

"I do need to go to the track later," Ethan said. "Get some practice in for the Lake Forest meet coming up. I don't know if there's time for the Depot, and to drive you home, and then to drive back to the school track."

I had an even better idea. "I'll go with you to school after the Depot. Then you can drive me home after practice, okay?" I knew Jack's football team would be practicing at the school field—maybe I'd get to see him there.

"Aren't you tired?" Ethan asked.

"A little," I answered honestly, "but I'm so excited about being back home, I feel energized." What I didn't tell him was that the thought of finally seeing Jack after a whole year away was enough to make me lose sleep for a week.

"Then the Depot it is," Ethan said, turning right at the intersection.

I didn't expect Ethan to say anything else. After all, it was Jack who was the charming, witty brother. Ethan was the quiet one. And since he and I had started high school, we'd stopped talking as much as we had when we were little kids. I guessed it was mostly my fault. Before I had even hit the ninth grade, I had a full-blown crush on Jack, and whenever I

28

saw Ethan, I'd bombard him with questions about his brother: Where was Jack? Who was he with? When would he be home? Ethan had probably just gotten tired of my questions.

But this time he surprised me. "You know, I never told you this, but I really admire you for getting out of Winnetka for a year," he said.

"It was fun and scary at the same time," I said. "And even though I had a blast and met a lot of new people, I still really missed—well, I missed everybody."

"Maybe I'll get my chance to travel soon, see the world. You know, the Chandlers have lived in Winnetka for more than a hundred years. Same house, same town, same church, same schools. I plan to be the first Chandler son to break out."

It was weird the way Ethan spoke about his family. The Chandlers this, the Chandlers that, as if he didn't feel he was really a member of the richest family in Winnetka. That was so unlike Jack, who seemed more than comfortable with his status.

"What about Jack?" I asked, staring out the window. "Doesn't he want to travel, too?"

"I don't think so. Jack's pretty happy right where he is. Captain of the wrestling team, quarterback of the varsity football team. He'll probably get accepted by Northwestern University for next year. Then he'll join the same fraternity that my father was in and my grandfather before him. Why would Jack want to leave?"

"But you do?"

"Maybe it's because I'm the second son. I'm not going to become president of the Chandler Tool and Die Company—Jack will. I mean, I could be part of the company if I wanted to, and there are even some shares set aside for me, but I'd always be in Jack's shadow if I stayed. Kind of like I am now."

I didn't know how to respond. What he said was absolutely true. Ethan had always been in Jack's shadow, at school and at home. He couldn't compete with Jack—he didn't have his looks or his charm, and he didn't seem to care about how he dressed most of the time. Only a year separated them, and yet they were worlds apart. I could see why Ethan would want to leave.

"So where do you want to travel to?" I asked lightly.

"First Germany," Ethan said as he continued to drive. "I took German because that's the language of science. I can answer just about any physics, chemistry, or math question in German. But I'm not sure I could order dinner in German, or tell the dry cleaner to get the stains out of my shirt, or ask for directions. I wish I were better at the real-life stuff of the language."

"Maybe you should switch to French," I suggested. "It's pretty easy to master, and it sounds really cool even when you're saying something silly like *'J'ai un crayon bleu.'*"

"Hey, French does sound a lot cooler than German. What did you just say?"

"I have a blue pencil."

"No way. Really? That sounded great. Maybe I should sign up for French," he said. "Somehow whenever I say something in German, it sounds like I'm yelling at the dog."

We both laughed, and I realized that for the past few minutes I hadn't thought of Jack once. I felt more relaxed than I had for the past week, worrying about seeing Jack, what I would say, what he would say . . .

I'd forgotten how easy it was to be with Ethan. Of course, that shouldn't have been a surprise. We had been best friends when we were little. We were the same age and had played together after school. Jack was usually off with his friends and didn't pay any attention to us because we were a year younger than he was. A year seemed like a lot back then.

But when we started high school, Ethan and I had drifted apart. Everyone assumed that if a boy and a girl were hanging out together, they must be dating. And the thought that people might think that about me and Ethan had embarrassed me, so I kind of avoided him. It probably wasn't the nicest way to handle things, but I wanted to make sure that Jack knew I was available to go out with him—not that he'd ever asked me.

Now I realized I might have missed something by cutting Ethan out of my life. He might not be as muscular as Jack, or as popular, and he certainly didn't make my heart skip a beat the way just thinking about Jack did. But he wasn't the geeky science nerd that a lot of people thought he was, either. And as I looked at him again now, he didn't look at all like a geeky science nerd, either. He must have gotten contacts, because he wasn't wearing glasses, and I knew he needed to wear glasses to drive. He was sort of cute in a friendly way—and you could tell just by looking at him that he was nice.

And his voice sounded softer than I remembered, but firm, self-assured. It almost sounded sexy. *That must be because he's speaking English!* I told myself. It felt like years since I had heard an American voice.

Of course, the most important thing about Ethan was that he was Jack's brother, and being Ethan's friend gave me the perfect excuse to keep running into Jack at the Chandler mansion.

"If you did take French, I could help you with your French homework," I suggested. I pictured myself over at the Chandlers' several afternoons a week. Jack couldn't help but notice me then.

"I think you're doing a pretty good job helping me right now. How do you say hello?"

"*Bonjour.*"

"Now how about 'You are very pretty'?" He had stopped at a red light.

"Well, there are two ways to say that. If you're saying it to a close friend, you'd say, '*Tu es très belle.*' But the more formal way of saying it would be '*Vous etes très belle.*'"

"*Tu es très belle,*" he repeated, gazing directly in my eyes.

"*Merci,*" I said, feeling my cheeks flush.

In all the time we had spent together in our lives, Ethan had never looked at me quite that way. Suddenly I felt uncomfortable with the French lessons. I wanted to change the subject back to Jack.

Becky hadn't been able to give me much information on how Jack had spent the year while I was in Paris, aside from the fact that he still dated Lydia Joyner on and off. The more I knew about Jack Chandler, the more likely my plan to snag him was to succeed. And I couldn't wait to put my plan into effect as soon as possible.

The light changed, and we turned onto the highway. Thankfully, the awkward moment between us was over, and I wondered if I had imagined the whole thing. After all, I hadn't seen Ethan without his glasses before. Maybe that was the way he had always looked at me, and I had just never noticed.

With the top off the Jeep, it was too noisy to keep talking, so I shoved in the tape Ethan had sticking out of the cassette player—something old by Eric Clapton—and turned up the volume high.

Soon we were on the familiar streets of Winnetka—Tudor-style houses, big elm trees, redbrick sidewalks, fenced-in swimming pools, and tennis courts.

When I'd left Winnetka the year before, I had felt out of place there. How could I belong in a community where some living rooms were as big as basketball courts? Where moms never worked and wore white pleated tennis skirts all through the winter? Where vacationing inside the United States wasn't considered a vacation at all? Where having at least two homes was required? Where everyone got a car for their sixteenth birthday, and their college tuition was paid for by a trust fund or some wealthy, doting relative?

Of course I didn't belong.

My grandparents had been servants—a fact that Lydia Joyner took pleasure in reminding me of as often as possible, preferably in a crowd.

But I was proud of my dad. He was a busy environmental lawyer—which was why he was away on business, as he often was, fighting some toxic villain in federal court somewhere. He had taught me that how much money you had wasn't as important as the contribution you made to helping other people and helping to keep the earth a beautiful place. I doubted that Lydia Joyner would buy that argument for a minute.

Ethan pulled into the parking lot of the Depot and hopped out of the Jeep without even opening the door. He was already around to my side before I had unfastened my seat belt.

I let Ethan open the door of the Jeep for me. I didn't think he would have done that for Gerolyn. But for Gigi . . .

Ethan held the door open, and I walked in ahead of him. I quickly scanned the people at the tables. Even though Ethan had told me Jack was at football practice, I couldn't help myself. I had seen a lot of cars in the parking lot when we'd pulled in, so I wasn't surprised that the place was packed. It took me a long time to check out every table. I did it casually because I didn't want Ethan to guess what I was doing.

But of course Jack wasn't there. I recognized a few of the teenagers from school. There were also several families. In fact, all the tables were full. The Depot had only one waiter or waitress for each shift, and another person behind the counter who handled the orders to go.

"Since you're in a hurry, why don't we just get some shakes to go?" I suggested.

Ethan gave me a thankful look as we approached the takeout area. Andrew Barnes, a senior who worked with Ethan in the physics tutoring program, stood behind the counter and took our orders for two double chocolate chip milk shakes.

As I wandered over to the window to look at the street, I heard Andrew ask Ethan, "Who's that girl?"

"Gigi," Ethan said. "I mean, Gerolyn Pelka."

"No way. That can't be Gerolyn."

I turned around and faced Andrew. Then I gave him my mysterious smile.

"Wow!" he said.

*Thank you, Paris,* I said silently.

I couldn't wait to see Jack now. He'd see that I'd changed. I had become the kind of girl he couldn't ignore.

# Chapter Three

ETHAN AND I sipped our shakes as he drove us to the school grounds. I was just finishing my last slurp as Ethan parked the Jeep in the school lot. He grabbed his gym bag and jumped out. "Catch you later," he called over his shoulder as he jogged to the locker room door.

I walked to the bleachers and found a spot in the late-afternoon sun. I had a good view of football practice.

*Where is he? Where* is *he?* My heart was pounding as I shaded my eyes with my hand and scanned the field. Nothing. And then—suddenly—I saw a flash of blue uniform, and there he was. The boy of my Parisian dreams, standing there in the flesh. Jack Chandler.

Seeing Jack after a whole year of just staring at his picture sent my blood pressure sky high. He was so much more handsome now than he had been the year before—a fact that I would have found hard to believe if I hadn't seen it for myself. He was a little taller, and, although it was difficult to tell since he was in his padded football uniform, I thought he looked even more muscular. His face was leaner, more grown-up. Even though he was a senior—only a year older than the guys in my grade—he looked more like a college guy.

I watched as Jack threw some long passes. A few minutes later, Ethan, wearing his running shorts and a tank top, jogged over to his brother. He looked so lean and lithe next to Jack.

*Stay cool,* I told myself. I couldn't let Jack see the desire in my eyes. That would ruin everything. I reminded myself that I was no longer Gerolyn, desperate for any show of attention Jack might give me. I was Gigi now, an alluring young woman who would knock Jack off his feet—if he would only look my way.

Ethan was saying something to Jack, then pointed up to where I was sitting. I gave a little wave. I wanted to try my mysterious smile, but I figured I was too far away for it to have any effect. *Be patient,* I told myself. *You'll get your chance soon enough.*

I didn't have to wait long. Football practice was over, and Jack ran up the bleacher stairs. He pulled off his football helmet and ran his fingers through his damp hair.

I was glad I was sitting down, because Jack looked even more handsome than he had the last time I'd seen him—the night before I left for Paris . . . kissing Lydia . . .

I blocked that image out of my mind and concentrated on Jack Chandler as he looked now—now that he was going to be mine.

His face, with those green eyes, was flawless. His body was muscular, without a smidgen of fat. And his hair, several weeks overdue for a cut, was sun-kissed and soft—girls would give anything to run *their* fingers through it.

"This can't be the Gerolyn Pelka I once knew," Jack said with a smile.

I felt as though I would melt. But my plan called for keeping it together. "Hi, Jack," I said coolly. Then I gave him my mysterious smile. "Call me Gigi."

"Gigi? Sure. Great name," he said, sitting on the bleacher in front of me. "It suits you."

I could tell he was taking me in—subtly. He probably didn't want to be crude and look me up and down, as some of the rude boys at school did. And I could also tell he liked what he saw.

"So tell me about Paris. I've always wanted to go, but the time's never been right. Is it really as beautiful a city as they say it is?"

"More so," I said, giving him another mysterious

smile. Then I told him all about Paris and my trip to Greece.

Jack listened, not uttering a word, as if I were the most beautiful, most interesting girl on earth. He laughed when I told him about ordering calf's brains by mistake in a restaurant. Being with him was like my dream come true. Véronique had been right: Jack Chandler was going to be mine.

"Oh, I got the card you sent me," Jack said when I'd run out of things to say. "It was sweet of you to think of me, especially since you were so busy. I'm not much of a letter writer myself."

"You're more a man of action," I suggested boldly.

"I like to think so." He hesitated a moment, then said, "Would you like to go to the movies with me tonight?"

"I'd love to," I said with a smile.

My plan was working to perfection.

*September 1*
*Winnetka, Illinois*

*Dear Véronique,*
    *Merci! Merci! Merci!*
    *I cannot say thank you enough. You were so totally, absolutely right about everything. I've been home less than a day, and already I have a date with Jack.*

At first I was disappointed that he hadn't met me at the airport, but his brother, Ethan, was there. I think I mentioned Ethan to you once or twice, didn't I?

Ethan took me for ice cream, then drove me to school, where Jack was playing football—American football, not soccer. Jack hardly recognized me. I was wearing the outfit we bought together at Printemps, and I had done my makeup the way you showed me. I know I looked fantastic.

I gave him my mysterious smile, and he asked me out. It was as easy as you said it would be.

I can't believe how lucky I was to have gotten a tutor like you. Not only did you help me pass all my courses, you changed my life!

I will always be grateful to you.

Lots of love,
Gigi

P.S. I wish you were here with me now to help me pick out my outfit for my date tonight with Jack. I'll write again soon to let you know how everything went.

I finished my letter to Véronique and lay back on my bed.

What should I wear?

Definitely one of my Paris outfits. Actually, I couldn't imagine wearing *any* of my old clothes ever again. They were all too Gerolyn. Only my French clothes seemed right for Gigi.

Finally I decided on one of my favorite Paris outfits—a short navy blue flared dress with an embroidered vest and tights that picked up the colors in the vest.

I used some of the light face powder Véronique had bought for me, and bright red lipstick. Véronique had told me to concentrate on one or two features—my lips or cheekbones or eyes. It was more natural and more dramatic than wearing a lot of makeup.

"Hi," I said.

Jack stood waiting out on our landing. He was wearing a pair of olive-colored pleated pants and a beige polo shirt. His hair was damp, and I could smell the faint aroma of shampoo. He looked perfect.

"*Bonjour,*" Jack said. His eyes twinkled. "You look great."

"Thanks," I said, my head spinning. I wanted to pinch myself to make sure I wasn't dreaming. I was really, truly going on a date with Jack!

I grabbed my purse and followed Jack out to his mother's red Miata convertible. It was such a sporty, flirty kind of car—perfect for a cool guy like Jack.

"Do you mind if we ride with the top down?" Jack asked. "It's such a nice night."

"Not at all," I told him. "I love feeling the wind in my face." Not to mention my hair. The breeze would be sure to blow my hair back, giving Jack the perfect opportunity to admire its golden highlights. And I was hoping people from school would see me with Jack. Who could miss a bright red convertible?

I smiled as he came around to open the door for me.

"The car was riding a little low today," he said, bending down to test the rear tire. "I just want to make sure we don't get a flat." I watched as he pushed his finger against the rubber. "Nope," he said, getting up and walking back around. "Looks fine."

"Um . . . good," I said as I opened the door. What was the big deal about opening doors, anyway? I was a sophisticated woman now. I could open my own door.

I smiled to myself. *Date number one with Jack Chandler, here we go!* I settled into my seat, and we headed for the multiplex.

On the way there, Jack entertained me with stories of the past year at Winnetka High: the mouse in the cafeteria, the principal's very public divorce and remarriage to a young assistant teacher, the Winnetka Warriors' last-second championship victory over our archrival, St. John's.

43

As I listened to Jack's stories I realized that not only was Jack the best-looking guy in all of Winnetka, he was also the most fun to be around. There were none of those awkward moments where you have nothing to say, then you both blurt out something at the same time, and argue over who should go first.

By the time we pulled into the parking lot of the Winnetka Multiplex Cinemas, I was convinced that I had been right all along—even though Becky Cohen, my best friend in the world, had tried to convince me otherwise. Jack and I were meant for each other. We would be the premier couple at Winnetka High that year. I would be the envy of all the girls as Jack pulled into the school parking lot every morning with me in the passenger seat. I couldn't wait to see the expression on Lydia Joyner's face.

Jack let me choose which movie we would see, and I picked a French film I had already seen in Paris. It was a very romantic movie—perfect for our first date. When I had seen it the first time, I imagined that Jack and I were the young lovers, separated during World War II, and finally reunited after many painful years apart.

We sat in the back row. As the previews began, Jack whispered in my ear, "I can't believe you were so close for all these years—literally in my own backyard—and it took us this long to find each other."

*It took this long for you to find me,* I corrected him in my mind.

As the lights dimmed, Jack slipped his arm over the back of my seat. During the coming attractions, I felt his hand lightly brush my shoulder. At first I stiffened at his touch. I was so nervous—I had waited practically all my life for this moment, to be on a real date with Jack Chandler. Now he was making his move, and I was petrified.

I realized that was the old Gerolyn reacting.

I tried to imagine how Véronique would act in a situation like this. She would probably expect her date to want to touch her. And she would want him to. She would relax into his touch, which was exactly what I tried to do.

I leaned back against his shoulder. Jack seemed encouraged by my response, and he started to play with my hair. I was glad I had left it natural after I shampooed and conditioned it, so it felt soft and silky instead of sticky with mousse or gel. His fingers caressed my neck and slipped down to rub my shoulders in a gentle massage.

As much as I had daydreamed about what it would be like to be with Jack, I could never have imagined the way it actually felt now that it was really happening to me. At first his touch was like a high-voltage wire on my bare skin. It jolted me and sent my heart racing.

But then, when I relaxed, it was like lying on a beach with the gentle heat of the sun washing over my entire body.

The movie started, and we sat back to watch. But the people in front of us were very tall, and we couldn't read the subtitles. Jack didn't know what the characters were saying, so I whispered a translation in his ear. His hair smelled clean, and I caught a whiff of aftershave on his cheek.

At one point he turned his head just as I was leaning in to translate a love scene, and his lips brushed against mine.

It wasn't exactly a kiss. It was more like our mouths were just accidentally in the same place at the same time.

It caught me off guard, and I was so stunned by what had happened that I didn't feel a thing. I had imagined that my first kiss with Jack would be a momentous event, something like a 7.2 on the Richter scale. But this wasn't anything like that. Maybe my expectations had been too high. Of course, this wasn't a real kiss, I reminded myself as Jack turned back to the screen. I tried not to be disappointed. But I was.

"So, what did you think of the movie?" I asked as the final credits rolled.

"I think it would have made more sense if I understood French," he responded with a smile.

"Wasn't my translation good enough?"

"I'm sure it was. I just couldn't concentrate on the movie with you breathing in my ear."

"I'm sorry if I distracted you," I said playfully. "Next time we'll sit somewhere closer to the front so you can read the subtitles."

"Not if I can help it," Jack said with a devilish grin as we got into the convertible.

I thought about how our lips had brushed. How could I not have felt something? Jack was gorgeous and charming, and I had been in love with him practically forever. It must have been my fault. I hadn't been ready for it. But I'd be ready the next time.

"How about some ice cream at the Depot?" Jack suggested.

"Sure." For some reason I didn't want to tell him I'd just been to the Depot with his brother that afternoon. I didn't know why, since there wasn't anything wrong with two friends—neighbors—going for an ice cream. I guess I just didn't want to mention Ethan while I was with Jack. I didn't want Jack to think of me as the little girl who had played with his brother when they were growing up. That was Gerolyn, and I was Gigi now.

The Depot was packed. I recognized a few people, and, of course, everyone from school had to say hi to Jack. One boy stared at me as I passed until his date poked him in the ribs to get his attention back. I noticed that a couple of senior girls looked on enviously.

Four guys from the football team were polishing off double sundaes. "Hey, Jack, my man," one of them said, sliding over. "Wanna join us?"

I flinched. This was my first date with Jack. I wanted it to be our night—Jack and me, alone. I didn't want to spend it with a bunch of jocks talking about blocks and fumbles.

Fortunately Jack seemed to read my mind. "Another time, dude. Catch ya later." He steered me toward a booth in the back that had just been vacated.

It took at least fifteen minutes before the waitress even took our order. I knew it would be another half hour before our ice cream arrived.

But so what?

I was right where I wanted to be—with Jack, the most handsome guy in Illinois, on our first date.

"So then what happened?" Becky asked. It was Saturday morning, and I could picture her lying on her bed with the cordless phone pressed hard against her ear.

"We ate our sundaes, and he drove me home," I answered with a giggle.

"Don't hold out on me, girl," Becky admonished. "Did he kiss you?"

"Except for that nonkiss at the movies, no."

"Oh." Becky sounded disappointed.

"I think he wanted to when he walked me to my door, but I didn't give him the chance. Part of my plan is to play hard to get. Besides, I was afraid that if we started kissing, I'd lose my self-control, and the sophisticated Gigi would disappear in a puff of smoke, with plain old Gerolyn taking her place."

"So when are you seeing him again?" Becky asked.

"Well, he asked me out for tonight, but I told him I wanted to spend the night with my dad. I think that shocked him. I don't think Jack's ever been turned down by a girl before."

"Wow. I can't believe my best friend is actually going out with Jack Chandler."

I laughed. "Really, Becky, you make it sound like I'm dating a movie star or something."

The phone clicked—my call waiting—and I told Becky to hold on while I switched to the other call. It was Jack. I said a quick good-bye to Becky.

"Gigi." Jack's voice sounded even sexier than usual. "I know you want to have dinner with your father tonight, but I can't get you out of my mind. I was hoping you'd stop by after dinner—it doesn't matter how late—and say good night."

"Gee, Jack, I don't know what time we'll get

49

back from the restaurant. . . ." Playing hard to get was getting more and more difficult.

"It doesn't matter. I'll be waiting."

Dad took me to my favorite Chinese restaurant. It felt great to be home and to see Dad, but my mind kept drifting back to Jack, waiting for me on the pool terrace.

It was late when we got home, and Dad went straight to bed.

I went up to my room as if I were going to bed and waited for him to turn out his light. Then I quickly put on some lipstick, fluffed my hair, and sneaked out of the house.

I found Jack waiting for me in one of the lounge chairs by the pool. The only light came from the moon and the candles he had placed on the small tables.

He jumped up when he saw me. "I'm glad you came," he said, taking my hand. Soft music drifted out from the speakers built into the deck. "I love this song. Would you like to dance?"

I nodded.

Jack pulled me to him, and we started to slow-dance. "You're so beautiful," he murmured in my ear. "I've never felt this way about a girl before."

He was saying exactly what I wanted him to say. What I had dreamed he would say. And I was finally in his arms, dancing with him under the moonlight.

The candles flickered in the breeze. It was more romantic than I could have ever imagined. I looked up into Jack's green eyes and felt my knees go weak. He tilted my chin up and leaned down. I smelled his minty breath just before his lips touched mine.

Suddenly the terrace was bathed in bright light.

"Oops! Sorry." It was Ethan.

Jack was as surprised as I was. He pulled back, and I felt his arms drop away. "Ethan! What's your problem?"

"I heard voices, and I thought it might be burglars," Ethan said. "Sorry if I interrupted anything."

Jack gave his brother a dirty look, but Ethan seemed oblivious to his brother's hostile glare.

"Hi, Gigi," he said with a smile.

"Hi, Ethan."

Jack wrapped his arms around me again. But somehow the bright lights and Ethan's sudden appearance had changed my mood. A moment earlier, Jack had been about to kiss me. I could almost feel his mouth on mine as he nibbled my lips. I had waited an eternity for that moment, and I could tell that Jack was ready to pick up where he had left off—with Ethan standing right there.

But I was embarrassed that Ethan had caught us. I felt a flood of emotions I didn't understand. All I knew was that I had to get out of there. As much as I'd wanted to kiss Jack—to have Jack kiss me—I didn't feel like having any witnesses, especially not Ethan.

"I—I have to go now," I mumbled, shrugging out of Jack's grasp. Then I turned and ran home.

When I got upstairs to my bedroom, I kept the light off and looked out the window. I heard Jack and Ethan talking, but I couldn't make out what they were saying. Then Jack stormed into the house. Ethan sank down into one of the chairs. I got into my pajamas, then went to the bathroom to brush my teeth.

Ethan was still sitting on the terrace when I went to bed.

# *Chapter Four*

September 3
Winnetka

Dear Véronique,

I didn't think I'd be writing you again so soon, but something happened last night. I wish I could call you to talk to you about it. It was so confusing. But my dad would have a fit if I called you so soon after leaving Paris. So I'm writing instead.

Last night after dinner with my dad, I stopped by to see Jack. We danced under the moonlight, and Jack was just about to kiss me when Ethan—I mentioned him in my last letter—turned on the lights.

It wasn't just the interruption that upset me. It was how self-conscious I felt

with Ethan watching me and Jack together. Is that normal? I mean, feeling
weird like that? I felt as though Ethan
had caught us doing something wrong.
But how could it be wrong to kiss the
boy of my dreams?

Write soon and tell me what you
think.

I miss you!

Love,
Gigi

I felt better after I had finished my letter to
Véronique. Even though I knew it would take
days for her even to get my letter, and probably
over a week before I'd get a response from her
with her advice, just writing about what I was
feeling helped a lot.

When I woke up the next morning, I realized
I had dreamed about Jack. About kissing Jack.
About what would have happened if Ethan
hadn't interrupted us. It was so real, too. One of
those vivid, full-color dreams. It was a fantastic
dream—but not as fantastic as I knew the real
thing would be.

As I lay in bed reliving my dream, I heard a
car revving its engine outside. I looked out the
window in time to see Jack driving away in the
Jeep, his windsurfing equipment in the back.

Chances were he would be gone all day at the lake.

Maybe Dad and I could find an excuse to go down to the lake—a picnic, for example. But when I got downstairs, I found a note that said he had an unexpected meeting that morning. I also found a glass of fresh-squeezed orange juice in the refrigerator. Good old Dad.

I drank my juice and went back to bed. Véronique had emphasized the importance of beauty sleep. That was one beauty treatment even I could afford.

Tuesday morning, the first day of school, was chaos. Everyone was hugging and kissing as if they hadn't seen each other in years. Becky and I were in the same homeroom again—thank goodness. But we had spent most of Sunday afternoon together, looking at photos of my trip and talking about you-know-who, so we didn't have a ton of stuff to catch up on.

Ms. Van Bearle made several announcements about new school rules: no torn jeans, no tank tops—boys or girls—and no miniskirts. A few boys in the back row groaned. Ms. Van Bearle smiled at them. She was a pretty cool teacher.

"I have one more announcement to make," she continued. "The varsity football team is sponsoring a dance this coming Saturday night."

Becky and I looked at each other and grinned.

"That's it," Ms. Van Bearle finished, just as the first-period bell rang.

As Becky and I went our separate ways to class, I wondered if Jack would ask me to the dance. *Of course he will,* I told myself, hoping that if I believed it, it would come true.

When I got home from school on Monday, I found an envelope on the floor just inside the door with my name printed on it. I recognized the Chandler crest on the envelope and quickly ripped it open.

Inside was a card-size piece of stationery with only one line:

*See you tonight? 7:30? I'll be waiting. . . .*
*Jack*

How romantic.

Maybe we could pick up where we had left off when Ethan had interrupted us Saturday night.

After dinner I went upstairs and put on a bodysuit and a long, flowing skirt. I imagined how the skirt would flare when Jack twirled me around. Dad was so engrossed in his work at the computer he didn't even look up when I said I was going over to the Chandlers' for a while.

I was relieved to see that the Jeep wasn't in its usual spot when I crossed the courtyard toward the mansion. I hoped that meant that Ethan was out. Maybe Jack had made it clear that Ethan should stay clear of the pool. That was fine with me. I didn't want any interruptions—just me and Jack and the moonlight.

Jack was waiting for me, as he'd said he would be. Even after growing up next door to him, even after seeing him year after year, I was still struck by how handsome he was. When he smiled at me, I felt my heart skip a beat.

"I was afraid you wouldn't come," he said, getting up from the lounge chair. "I was afraid you wouldn't find the note and I'd have a lonely night without you."

A moment later Jack was taking me in his arms. Then I felt the gentle touch of his lips. I waited for the world to stop rotating on its axis. But it was not the kiss I had dreamed of so many times.

Actually, kissing Jack in real life wasn't at all like I had imagined it would be. I'd thought I would melt into his arms, that time would stand still. Instead, when his lips grazed mine, I felt a sense of triumph. My moment had finally arrived. Jack Chandler was kissing me! But there were no fireworks, only a warm sensation from my toes to the top of my head.

Of course, I hadn't kissed many boys before

Jack. And none of those kisses had been earth-shaking, either. Maybe this was just what kissing was like.

I'd have to write to Véronique and ask her.

The first week of school zipped by. Becky and I had several classes together, and we saw each other every day at lunch. I saw Jack most evenings. He took me out to dinner one night, bowling another, and one evening we spent dancing on the pool terrace in the moonlight.

It was the most romantic week of my entire life. But in all the time Jack and I had spent together, he'd never asked me to the dance. I wondered if he just assumed that we would go as a couple now that we were spending so much time together.

Several guys had asked me if I would go with them, and I'd turned them all down. By the time Friday rolled around, I was wondering if I had made a mistake. If Jack didn't ask me, then I would be stuck without a date. I didn't want Jack to think I couldn't get a date for the football team's back-to-school dance.

I wished I could talk to Véronique about all this. She was so much more experienced than I was. She would know what to do.

By Friday morning, I was panicked. Could Jack really ask someone else to the dance after he and I had spent practically every evening that week in each other's arms?

I was late to homeroom. Becky was already there, and I took my regular seat next to her. My expression said everything I was feeling.

"I take it he still hasn't asked you," she said sympathetically.

"No, but today's not over yet," I said hopefully.

I must have been really out of it, because I didn't even realize that Ms. Van Bearle had dismissed us until I felt Becky tugging at my sleeve. "Come on, sleepyhead," she said. "Time to wake up."

I smiled. "See you at lunch," I said to Becky as I let the flow of students carry me out into the hall.

The seniors had a different lunch period than the juniors, so I was surprised to see Jack at lunch a few hours later.

The noise level in the cafeteria dropped as he made his way over to our table and sat down next to me. I could feel everyone's eyes zeroing in on our table as Jack put his arm around my shoulder.

"I know it's late to be asking," he began, "but I was hoping you'd go to the dance with me tomorrow night."

I almost blurted out "Yes!" before I remembered that my plan called for me to be more aloof. Jack shouldn't have waited till the day before the dance to ask me. "I don't know. . . . Several guys have already asked me. . . ."

I watched as Jack's face fell into a gloomy frown.

"But I turned them all down."

Jack smiled, and I realized I enjoyed playing this game.

"I turned them down because Becky and I had already made plans to go to the movies."

Jack's face fell again, and I felt a surge of triumph. He was really disappointed.

Then I felt a sharp pain in my shin. Becky had kicked me— hard. "But I guess we can go another night. Right, Becky?" I said with a smile.

"Does that mean you'll go with me?" He broke into a wide grin.

"Yes, that's exactly what I mean."

"Great! I'll pick you up at eight. See you tomorrow, Gigi." Jack stood up and jogged out of the cafeteria. About a hundred pairs of eyes followed him, including mine.

"I can't believe these dresses!" Becky squealed as she looked from one of my Paris purchases to another. "They are incredible!"

It was late Saturday afternoon, and Becky and I were trying to decide what to wear to the dance that night. Becky was going with a couple of other girls who didn't have dates. A lot of guys went to the dance solo, and Becky wasn't going to stay home just because no one had asked her to go.

"Can I really borrow one for tonight? You are the best, best friend in the world!" Becky held up one dress after another as she stood in front of my full-length mirror.

I had already selected the dress I wanted to wear. It was a slinky black sheath. It was more elegant than what most of the girls would be wearing, but that was fine. I wanted to look different, more sophisticated. I knew Jack would appreciate it—after all, he was a pretty sophisticated guy himself.

"I think I'll be the lady in red," Becky said, holding up a red silk minidress. "I want to attract some attention tonight."

"Oh, really? And who's the lucky guy?" I asked, although I had a pretty good idea who he was.

Before I'd left for France, Becky and I had listed the ten cutest guys in school, the ten smartest, and the ten funniest. Andrew Barnes had ended up on all three of Becky's lists.

"You know," Becky said, pressing her lips together, "I think Andrew is just shy. I probably should have asked him to the dance myself, but I chickened out."

The phone rang. I waited till the third ring to pick up.

"Hello?" I said.

"Hi, Gigi. This is Jack."

"Hi, Jack," I said as if I always got calls from gorgeous guys.

"I, uh, can't pick you up," Jack said. "I'm really sorry, but I sprained my ankle playing football and I have to get it taped up. I'll meet you at the dance, okay? Ethan'll pick you up and drive you there for me."

"He doesn't have to do that. I can get a ride with Becky and the girls."

"No, really, I feel terrible about this. Please let Ethan take you. He'll keep you company till I arrive. Besides, I don't want you getting swept off your feet by another guy before I get there."

"But doesn't Ethan have a date?"

"Are you kidding? Ethan date?"

I could think of a bunch of girls who would have gone to the dance with Ethan if he'd asked them. Even though he was kind of shy and quiet, he was interesting to talk to once he got going.

But if Jack wanted Ethan to drive me to the dance, that was fine with me.

"Okay, what do you think?" Becky asked, parading around the room a few hours later. We had done our hair and our makeup, but Becky was still agonizing over her outfit.

I remembered what Véronique had taught me about using accessories. I grabbed a wide black belt off another dress and handed it to her. "Here, try this."

The belt pulled the outfit totally together. Becky twirled in front of the mirror, and the skirt of the dress fluttered out.

"No way will Andrew Barnes be able to resist you tonight," I said.

"You're sure it looks good?" Becky asked, insecurity written all over her face.

"Yes, you look absolutely fantastic," I assured her. "When Andrew sees you, he won't know what hit him."

"Earrings!" Becky said urgently, rifling through my jewelry box until she found the pair she was looking for. "Can I borrow these?"

As Becky struggled with the posts we heard the honk of Ethan's Jeep. It was eight o'clock on the dot.

Becky wished me good luck with Jack as the doorbell rang, and we ran down the stairs. My dad opened the door to find Ethan standing there, holding a small plastic florist's box. He was wearing black jeans, a button-down shirt, and an Italian suit jacket—and boy, did he look great.

I stopped and stared, holding my breath.

"Man, oh, man," Becky whispered behind me. "Gigi, I think you've got a thing for the wrong brother."

Ethan made elegance look so natural. Even when he combed his fingers through his hair, I wasn't thinking, "He really needs a haircut," like I usually did. Instead I was thinking about how it would feel to run my own hands through that soft, silky hair. And when he unconsciously straightened the cuff of his shirt, I thought it was the sexiest movement I had ever seen.

*Stop it!* I told myself. *Jack is waiting for you.*

I felt a strange sensation in my throat, and I was afraid to speak. I smiled, testing Ethan to see if he was angry with me for taking up his evening—an evening he probably would have preferred to spend running the Green-leaf trail.

He smiled back, just enough to let me know everything was going to be okay.

I must have stood at the bottom of the stairs for a long time, because the next thing I knew, Becky was pushing me forward.

"I'm so glad you're going with Ethan," my dad said brightly. "You'll have a wonderful time."

"She's not exactly going with me, sir," Ethan corrected. "She's really Jack's date."

My dad looked baffled as he stared at Ethan. He glanced past Ethan and looked at me, then back at Ethan again, clueless.

"Jack sprained his ankle," Ethan politely explained to my father. "He asked me to drive

Gerol—Gigi to the dance for him."

"Oh, okay," my dad said slowly, taking off his reading glasses. "Well, I guess, have a good time with Jack, then."

Ethan held out the florist's box. Inside was a white orchid corsage with a red ribbon.

"Um, thanks . . . it's from Jack?"

"I know Jack would have bought you flowers if he were taking you," he said. "So I thought I'd do the same . . . for him, I mean."

"This is so beautiful," I said, touching the pretty white orchid. "And so thoughtful, Ethan. But I feel bad, ruining your night. If you'd rather stay home, I'll understand. I can catch a ride with Becky."

Ethan shook his head. "I told Jack I'd take you. I don't go back on my word."

My dad took off his glasses and rubbed them against his shirtsleeve. I could tell he was totally confused.

But then again, so was I.

Why was Ethan doing this? Why did Jack feel that I had to have an escort to the dance when I was his date? There was so much about Jack and Ethan that I didn't understand. Of course, being an only child, I didn't know much about having a brother or sister. Maybe this was just one of those sibling things.

"Here, let me pin this on you," Becky said, taking the orchid from my hand. "You should really get going. You guys don't want to be late. And I have to pick up Mandy and Ellen in ten minutes."

She fussed with the flower, the pin, and the top of my dress while Ethan and I looked at each other. His eyes were unreadable.

"Gerolyn, I'm confused," my dad said. "You're going to the dance with Jack, but Ethan's here now. So . . . who's going to drive you home?"

"Uh, I'll just . . . get a ride from . . . uh . . ."

"I'll drive her home," Ethan said firmly.

"Or maybe Jack will," I blurted out.

"All right, Gerolyn. Just make sure you get home safely," my dad said.

"Thanks, Dad. And Becky, I'll see you at the dance."

I hugged both my dad and Becky good-bye and then followed Ethan out to the Jeep.

"So you're not mad at me?" I asked a few minutes later as we drove down the private road that led out to the main street.

He shook his head. "Why would I be mad at you?"

"For lousing up your evening. I thought you didn't like school dances. You never went to any before."

"You're right. I never did care much for dances. Too many people in one place. I'm more a one-on-one kind of guy. But this is different, Gigi. I'm just being a good brother. And a friend to you." He paused for a long moment. "I'll be honest with you. I'm not real happy with this arrangement, but I agreed to it. So let's drop it, okay?" he said, his eyes fixed on the road.

"Yeah, sure, if that's what you want." *This is so unlike Ethan,* I thought as we drove the rest of the way in stony silence. *He's usually so easygoing. Something must be eating him.* But I was too keyed up about being Jack's date to really analyze what Ethan was going through. He was a self-sufficient guy. He'd eventually work out whatever was bugging him.

Ethan parked the Jeep in the school lot. He switched off the ignition and leaned against the steering wheel. "Gigi, before you go inside, I have to tell you something." He took a deep breath. "I think Jack's the wrong guy for you."

"Ethan!" I said, surprised. "I know what I want, and I—"

"Let me finish," he interrupted. "I know how you feel about Jack. You've never tried to disguise your feelings for him around me. We've always been honest with each other, and that's why I want to tell you some things about Jack that you may not know."

"Ethan, I appreciate your concern," I said, growing annoyed. "But I can take care of myself."

Ethan stared out the front window of the Jeep at the cornfields beyond the track. "I wish I believed that. But I don't think you're a match for Jack. He's a lot more experienced—"

This was getting downright insulting. Just because I was Ethan's age didn't mean I was as naive as he was. "I don't need you to look out for me. I'm a big girl, Ethan," I said, impatient to get out of the Jeep and into Jack's arms on the dance floor.

Ethan finally got the not-so-subtle hint. He got out of the Jeep without another word.

We walked quietly toward the gym. Suddenly we were swept up in a crowd of party-goers gathered outside the door to the gym.

"Ethan! What are you doing here?" somebody shouted out, and he was swallowed up into a sea of jackets and bright-colored dresses.

As I searched the area for a sign of Jack, I felt somebody pull at my arm. "Gerolyn Pelka, is that really you?" Raymonda Dabaday asked. She was a Haitian-born girl from my French class who'd taught me a lot of French slang before I'd left for Paris.

"It's Gigi now," I said distractedly, looking around at the mass of people. *Jack said he might be late,* I told myself. *He's probably not here yet.*

"Whatever. Boy, you sure have changed," she said.

"Yeah, well . . ." I arched my neck, trying to get a glimpse of Ethan. He was supposed to be my escort, but he had abandoned me—some friend.

"Who are you here with?" Raymonda asked, pulling me through the doors to the gym.

"I don't know. I mean, I guess I'm with Ethan Chandler. No, Jack Chandler, really. Well, I'm not sure."

She giggled. "That's great. I came by myself, too."

Raymonda and I entered the gym, which looked more like a nightclub than the sweaty-smelling torture chamber it usually was. The basketball hoops had been tucked up nearly to the ceiling, the bleachers were stacked against the wall, the lights were turned down low, and a big Winnetka Warriors banner hung over the center line. Balloons, streamers, and handmade posters were stapled to the walls. Punch and snacks were piled on a table at one end of the gym, and the chaperons huddled in chairs at the other.

The band was playing a popular dance tune, something with a quick beat.

Raymonda snapped her fingers. "Wow, look at him go!" she said, pointing to the clump of dancers in the center of the room.

I followed her gaze and felt my mouth go dry when I saw Jack.

"He's amazing," Raymonda said. "Then again, he's great at everything he does."

"Yeah, I guess so," I answered quietly. He wasn't dancing like a guy who'd just sprained his ankle, that was for sure. Jack probably went to the most expensive doctor in Winnetka—one who'd been able to work wonders with his injury.

Raymonda drifted off to talk to a group of girls near the snack table, and I rehearsed what I would say when Jack came over to me.

The year before, Gerolyn Pelka would have felt self-conscious standing alone at a school dance. But after a year in Paris I had enough self-confidence not to worry about what other people would think. After all, I was dressed to kill, and I knew I looked hot. Jack wouldn't be able to resist me once he realized I was there—which, by the looks of it, might take some time.

He was totally engrossed in his dancing. I didn't mind waiting, watching him move so fluidly. It was as if he had become part of the music, a physical embodiment of the rhythmic beat. No doubt about it, Jack Chandler was a great dancer. I thought about the previous Saturday night, dancing with him on the moonlit pool terrace . . .

A group of people backed away from Jack, giving him more room to move around in. And that was when I saw who his partner was.

Lydia Joyner.

Lydia was facing Jack, her fingers snapping in time to the music, her shiny hair bouncing with every sway of her head. She was wearing a low-cut dress that showed plenty of cleavage. A lot of guys were almost drooling as they watched from the sidelines, their jaws hanging open.

Lydia might have Jack for this dance, I thought, watching them move around the dance floor, but he was my date.

Wasn't he?

As the song ended I made my way to the snack table and snatched a can of soda from an ice-filled bucket.

My mind drifted back to what Ethan had been trying to tell me out in the parking lot. Were there things about Jack I didn't know? Well, of course there were. Jack and I had said hardly two words to each other growing up. Sure, I'd admired him from afar, but there was certainly tons of stuff about Jack I didn't know. Stuff I would learn now that we were spending more time together.

A lot of time . . .

The music started up again, and Jack pulled Lydia into an extravagant twirl, making her short dress fly around her like butterfly wings.

It was obvious how much fun Jack was having with Lydia. I hated to admit it, but they looked good together. I quickly shoved that thought away. Jack had invited me to the dance. And Jack and I would look great together—as soon as we were in fact together.

I put down my soda and moved toward the dance floor. I wasn't going to wait for Jack to notice me. That was how Gerolyn would have handled the situation. But Gigi would take action. The next dance would be ours, I would make sure of that.

I was walking up to Jack as the music ended, but I wasn't fast enough. Jack had already switched partners with one of his buddies from the football team. He ended up with Karen Haupt, a cheerleader who had been dancing with the team's fullback.

"Wanna dance?" someone asked from behind my back.

It was Andrew Barnes.

"Sure," I said, "I'd love to."

Maybe when Jack saw me dancing with Andrew he'd remember what he said on the phone about not wanting me to get swept off my feet by another guy.

Not that Andrew was much competition for Jack. Andrew, like Ethan, had a reputation for being something of a science nerd. But, like Ethan, Andrew had changed a lot during the year I'd been away. I was happy to see that he'd ditched the plastic pocket protector he'd worn religiously all through freshman year. He actually looked quite handsome in his blue blazer and gray slacks.

Andrew guided us to an empty spot on the dance floor, and we began to dance to a slow, dreamy song.

"You look great," Andrew said, holding me at arm's length. "I hardly recognized you when you came into the Depot with Ethan—not that you didn't look good before. You must have had a blast in Paris."

"Yeah, it was pretty fun," I said, scanning the crowd. I didn't want Becky to freak if she came in and saw us, even though we were dancing about a foot apart. "So . . . uh, Andrew, what did you do all last year while I was away?"

"Nothing much. Ethan and I took first place at the science fair semifinals. But you probably knew that," he said. And then he hesitated. "You came with Ethan tonight, right?"

"Yeah, but I can't find him." It was easier to say that than to try to explain the real situation. "So, who'd you come with?"

"Nobody," he admitted awkwardly. He glanced around the dance floor, then shrugged. "Is, um . . . Becky here tonight?"

"She will be soon," I said.

"Who's she coming with?" he asked, his cheeks flaming.

I looked at his eyes, and a sudden realization

shot through me. He liked Becky as much as she liked him. "She's coming with some girlfriends. She doesn't have a date."

"C'mon, I'm sure she had at least a dozen guys ask her."

I shook my head. "No one asked her," I added pointedly.

He sighed, a mixture of relief and longing. "I wanted to ask her, but I figured she already had a date for the dance."

Just then Becky walked through the door to the gym. I waved at her and disengaged myself from Andrew. "I see Becky over there. Why don't you go ask her to dance?"

"Wow, thanks, Gerolyn—I mean Gigi. I will."

He dropped my hands and sprinted away, clearing a path through the crowd of dancers with ease. I smiled as I imagined how happy Becky was going to be.

But now I was standing alone in the middle of the dance floor. That wasn't exactly how I'd imagined the evening would be. At this point, though, I would have welcomed a dance even with Ethan—despite our fight in the parking lot. But he was dancing with Raymonda, laughing at something she whispered in his ear.

I walked purposively toward the enormous punch bowl, picked up an empty glass, and thought about my options. I could sit with the chaperons. I could find someone who wasn't dancing and start up a conversation. I could pretend I had to fix my makeup and spend half an hour in the bathroom. Or I could walk out the door and hitchhike home.

The song ended again, but I didn't turn around to face the spot where I knew Jack was. I didn't want to look like an expectant puppy at the side of the dance floor.

I filled my punch glass and then absently filled another.

"You're not having a good time." Ethan startled me as he came up behind me. He took one of the glasses of punch from my hands.

"I'm having a fine time," I lied, thinking that Ethan's words sounded too much like "I told you so."

"Well, would you like to dance?"

"It's my dance, Ethan," Jack said, suddenly appearing. He put his arm around my shoulder. "If that's all right with you, Gigi."

Was it ever!

# Chapter Five

JUST ONE WORD from Jack and everything tilted back to perfection.

Jack took my arm, and the rest of the world disappeared. Gone were the angry thoughts, the desire to go home.

"I just saw you this minute. Have you been here long?" Jack asked, guiding me to the center of the dance floor.

"Not very long," I answered, although the past half hour had seemed like an eternity.

*But it was worth the wait,* I thought as he pulled me close.

"You're the most beautiful girl here," he whispered in my ear, nuzzling my neck. "And I'm the luckiest guy."

Absolute heaven.

"How's your ankle?" I asked.

Jack shook his head. "I can't hear you!" he shouted over the loud music.

The band started a fast tune with a driving beat, and Jack let go of me. We got totally wild. He spun me around and around till I was dizzy. Then he pulled me in close, and I could feel his heart beating against my own. As the song came to an end I couldn't wait for the next one.

*Please be a slow song,* I silently prayed.

But before I had a chance to hear the first note of the next song, Jack was rushed by two girls at the same time—both begging a dance. Jack took the hand of the first girl, promised to dance with the other one later, and gave me an "I'll see you later" wink.

I felt like a complete fool.

Jack danced those two dances without me. Then he danced with Lydia again. Then he danced with Karen Haupt.

All this with a sprained ankle, no less.

I took a seat next to Raymonda on some chairs by the chaperons.

"I'm pooped," she announced. I could tell Raymonda was perfectly happy sipping her punch and watching the dancers.

I wished I were pooped. But I couldn't be tired—all I'd done for the past hour was watch Jack dance with every girl who'd asked. I wondered if Jack would even notice if I left. Well, I'd soon find out.

I said *au revoir* to Raymonda and quickly headed for the exit. That might have been the smartest move I'd made all night, because Jack suddenly broke free of all his "obligations" and caught up with me.

"I'd give anything for it to be just you and me," he whispered in my ear.

"Would you really?" I asked coolly, heading toward the door.

"Yes, I would," he said. "The football team is sponsoring this dance. As starting quarterback, I have a responsibility to make it a success. If I danced every dance with you, like I wanted to, I'd offend a lot of people." Jack paused for a moment, stroking my cheek. "I'm sorry if this wasn't the best date for you. Let me make it up to you. C'mon, let's go outside and talk. Just you and me. I wish we weren't even at this dance. All day I've been thinking about how much I want to spend time with you, alone."

"I thought you were playing football all day," I corrected.

"When I wasn't concentrating on the game, I was thinking how it would have been a lot nicer to take a walk in the park, just the two of us."

My annoyance was slowly melting. Jack was my dream guy. I should have been happy he'd asked me to the dance. That should have been enough. Besides, it was close to impossible to stay mad at a guy who had the sexiest smile in the world. And Jack was certainly using every megawatt of that smile on me right then.

"Are you telling me the truth, Jack?" I asked, my resistance giving way.

"Scout's honor. Come on. Let's disappear for a while," he suggested, lightly kissing my ear, or rather, kissing the earring in my ear. "No one will notice. And who cares if they do? Doesn't this crowd make you feel claustrophobic?"

"Totally," I admitted. "Where do you want to go?"

"Let's just take a walk," he said.

He was limping slightly, and I noticed that the fabric of one pant leg was bunched around the protective bandage on his ankle.

"Maybe not a walk," Jack said, shaking his leg so the cuffs of his pants covered the bandage again. "Maybe we could just find a quiet place to be alone."

Yes! This was definitely a plan.

Me and Jack. Together.

Alone.

"Why don't you go on ahead toward the track? I'll get us some sodas. I'm feeling kind of dehydrated after all that dancing."

He gave me a soft kiss on the mouth. His lips lingered on mine, and whatever fragments of anger I had left quickly vanished. "I'll be right behind you," he promised.

I was about to go outside when I saw Becky

and Andrew on the dance floor. They were dancing so close, it was as though they were stuck together with glue.

*All right, Becky!* I silently cheered her on. *Go for it!*

I searched the dance floor for Ethan, but he was nowhere to be seen. Maybe he'd gotten bored and left. After our almost-fight in the parking lot, I guessed he wasn't planning on driving me home—not that I'd need him to, since Jack would.

Jack . . .

Where was he?

*How long does it take to grab two sodas?* I thought as I scanned the refreshment area.

I circled the dance floor, and finally glimpsed him. A crowd had backed off to watch Jack dance to a fast-paced song with another girl. She had probably ambushed him on his way to getting our sodas, I thought. I stood at the edge of the crowd, watching him twist and shake.

The crowd clapped and shrieked to the beat of the music, all the time watching Jack in action. Jack appeared to be in his element, thriving on all the attention he was getting. I could tell that having an audience spurred him on.

But his audience also made it impossible for us to be alone. I needed some air. Maybe a walk would help clear my head. I turned toward the exit door and pushed on the door handle. It opened silently, and I stepped outside.

I found myself on the outdoor basketball courts, under a thick haze of gray smoke. This was obviously where the smokers hung out. The smell reminded me of the cafés in France.

I walked past the smokers, past the out-of-bounds line, and down the slope to the track. I could still faintly hear the music from the party in the gym behind me.

*Brrr.* I shivered. It was chilly outside, and my lightweight dress didn't offer much protection from the wind. I hadn't thought to bring a jacket. *Maybe Jack will lend me his jacket—if he ever gets out here,* I thought. I had goose bumps on top of goose bumps on my arms and legs.

Suddenly I heard the sound of someone walking across the grass behind me. I let out a breath I hadn't known I was holding. I quickly turned around, and the smile on my face faded when I realized it was Ethan walking toward me, not Jack. And he was holding two cans of soda.

"Where's Jack?" I asked slowly.

Had he really ditched me?

"He hurt his ankle," Ethan said with a shrug.

"What? Again?"

"He shouldn't have been dancing on it," he

added, handing me a cold can of soda.

"Is he okay?" I asked, already heading back to the gym. I was Jack's date. Even if we hadn't spent much time together that evening, I thought I should be with him if he was hurt. Besides, I was pleased to have an excuse to get away from Ethan. I wasn't in the mood for Ethan to rub my nose in the fact that Jack hadn't treated me very well that evening—as he had hinted in the parking lot earlier.

"No, don't go," Ethan said, slipping his arm around my shoulders to stop me. "It wasn't all that bad. Besides, he's already being taken care of. Coach Greer is driving him home. Coach said if Jack's careful, he'll still be able to play next week's game. He just lost his balance and landed on the ankle the wrong way. It happened at the refreshment table."

I hid a smile. Not that I was happy about Jack's being injured, but if it had happened at the refreshment table, that meant Jack had been on his way out to me. He'd planned to get us some drinks—the dance was just a detour, as I had suspected.

"Poor Jack," I said.

"You know, the team doctor warned him not to come tonight, but Jack said he didn't want to disappoint anybody."

I didn't say anything.

"He asked me to come out here," Ethan said,

opening his can of soda. "He said you'd be here waiting for him."

Jack thought of everything. Even when he was in pain, he was considerate enough to make sure I didn't wait out in the cold for him.

A gust of wind blew across my bare shoulders, and my fingers shook as I opened my can.

"Gigi, you're freezing," Ethan said.

"A little," I admitted, trying to hide my shivers.

He pulled off his jacket and helped me into it.

I pulled the jacket tightly around me—it was still warm from Ethan's body heat. Then I followed him out into the middle of the field. The music from the gym floated across the distance to us, sounding very far away.

Ethan lifted his can of soda and touched it against mine.

"To Jack's ankle getting better," I said.

"He'll be fine," Ethan assured me. "Let's toast your coming home instead." We sipped our sodas, then Ethan held his hand out to me. "Come here."

"Why? What are you doing?"

"Would you like to dance? This is a great song. If Jack were here, he'd dance with you," he whispered as he took the can out of my hand and put it on the ground next to his. "I don't want your evening to be a total disappointment."

I didn't move. Ethan was acting so weird.

And suggesting that dancing with him would be anything like dancing with Jack was ludicrous.

"Duty date's over, Ethan," I said at last. "You can take me home. Go wherever you'd planned to go before Jack roped you into babysitting me."

"How about dancing with me because I ask you to—for me, not Jack?"

For some reason I felt tense at the thought of dancing with Ethan. I reminded myself that there was no reason to be nervous. I'd danced with Ethan before at parties.

But this was different somehow.

"Jack was supposed to meet me out here," I said. "I'm his date. He should be out here with me."

Ethan sighed, taking both my hands and pulling me to him. "You're right, he should. But I'm here instead." He held me tight.

I pictured Jack in my mind. The way he held me when we danced on the pool terrace. The way he kissed me—

"I know you're thinking of Jack," Ethan said sharply, interrupting my thoughts.

*How did he know that?* I asked myself silently. *Can he read my mind? Or am I just so transparent?*

"I know you, Gigi. You're thinking of Jack because he's your date tonight. Once you make up your mind to be with someone, you're faithful to a fault. You're so loyal, so intense."

Ethan's breath was warm, his arms around me strong, his voice low and soothing. "Come on, Gigi. We're friends."

As we danced I closed my eyes and tried to imagine I was in Jack's strong arms. I pretended it was Jack's fingertips that stroked my hair . . . *his* cheek pressed against mine.

But I couldn't smell Jack's distinctive aftershave. I could only smell Ethan and autumn—citrus mixed with damp grass, touched with the scent of burning leaves.

This wasn't the easiest place to dance, either. My heels kept getting caught in the holes made by the football players' cleats earlier that day. But Ethan was a surprisingly good dancer. At one point he twirled me around, and his jacket slid off my shoulders and fell to the ground.

I stopped to pick it up—it was obviously an expensive suit coat, and I didn't want it to get dirty.

"Forget about it," Ethan whispered, his voice deeper than usual. He continued dancing.

I no longer felt cold, even though the temperature was sinking fast.

Although I tried, I couldn't pretend Ethan was Jack. He felt totally different from Jack. I knew I wasn't dancing with Jack. I was dancing with Ethan . . . and having a great time.

"Ethan . . . ," I began as we continued to sway to the muffled music. Dancing with Ethan made me feel so good, so unexpectedly wonderful.

Then Ethan leaned his head toward mine, as if to kiss me. And I completely forgot everything I'd been about to say.

"Ethan, no." I quickly came to my senses, gently pushing him away.

"Shh, it's okay," Ethan whispered. Then he kissed me on the forehead.

Just the slightest pressure of his lips.

Magic.

And suddenly we were kissing each other. Really kissing each other.

Our lips brushed against each other softly at first, then with more and more urgency. I squeezed my eyes shut so tightly I felt the stars against my lids. I heard fireworks roar against my ears. I was soaring. . . .

Ethan lifted his head slightly. He looked at me strangely for a second, and then pulled me to him for another mind-exploding kiss.

Finally he took a step back.

I was stunned. *How can I go from wanting Jack so desperately to kissing Ethan like that in just one night?* I wondered. *I have got to get a grip.*

"Gigi . . ." He seemed about to say something

important. Something I didn't want to hear.

"Ethan, I'm dating your brother. Remember? We . . . we just got carried away. Let's leave it at that, okay?" I tried to sound firm, but my body begged for another of his kisses. I knew I'd probably hurt Ethan's feelings, but I had no other choice.

There was silence for a few moments.

"Come on, I'll take you to Homer's," Ethan finally suggested.

"Huh?"

"Homer's. You gotta remember that place. The underage dance club out on Green Bay Road."

"I know the place, Ethan. I just don't know why we should go there." I picked up his jacket from where I'd let it fall on the damp grass.

"I don't know—to have some fun?" He didn't sound very convincing. "The whole football team's meeting there after the dance. That's where Jack would take you. I'm just filling in for my brother, remember?"

"Ethan, stop it! You're not Jack. Don't tell me about what Jack would do if he were here. What would you do?"

"If you were my date?" he asked. Then he stared at me a long time. "I'd take you back to the Depot," he said at last. "It would take us an hour to get them to make us two orders of fries and sodas. But it would still be better than going to Homer's. And the Depot would let us hang around all night without hassling us."

I smiled, relieved Ethan was back to talking without that strange huskiness in his voice. Relieved he wasn't going to kiss me again, that he was walking me to the parking lot and acting as if we were just friends.

And that was just how I wanted it.

# Chapter Six

"I F I WATCH one more cartoon, I'm going to scream!" I said, grabbing the remote control.

Jack tried to get it back, and we wrestled playfully on the couch in the Chandlers' study. We ended up all tangled together in the lamb's wool afghan that had been hanging on the back.

It was Sunday morning, and I had come over to see how Jack was doing. I was feeling more than a little guilty about having kissed Ethan the night before. And then, after the dance, Ethan and I had hung around the Depot for hours, talking and laughing and having a great time. Andrew and Becky had stopped by around one o'clock, and the four of us spent another hour together.

When Ethan took me home, I'd gone directly

91

to my bedroom window to see if Jack's bedroom light was still on.

But he must have already gone to bed.

Only Ethan's light had remained on . . . long into the night.

I hadn't been able to fall asleep for hours. I'd kept thinking about how great it had felt to kiss Ethan. Well, of course, I'd been trying to imagine I was kissing Jack, not Ethan, but somehow I was having a hard time doing it. I wished I could just forget all about Ethan and pick up with Jack where we'd left off.

Which was exactly what we were trying to do.

Jack put his arms around me, and suddenly I didn't care if I had to watch cartoons for the rest of my life, so long as my eyes were on Jack and his lips were on mine.

When Jack's lips touched my mouth, I waited for the fireworks to go off in my head and erase the memory of Ethan's passionate kisses.

I waited.

And waited.

And waited.

Our lips were pressed tightly together, but aside from that I felt nothing.

Nothing at all.

Just then Ethan walked into the room with a bulging grocery bag. Embarrassed at being caught in such a position, I started to get up, but Jack held me down.

"Aren't you comfortable?" he asked in a sexy voice.

I nodded. Even though kissing Jack wasn't as thrilling as I had thought it would be, it still made me feel good. And sitting with Jack on the sofa was one sure way to make Ethan understand that I was committed to my relationship with Jack and not at all interested in whatever dirt he wanted to dish on his brother. Or in any more of his kisses . . .

Yes, Jack was definitely right. I was comfortable. There was no reason to get up just because Ethan had entered the room. Why shouldn't Ethan see us like this? I was Jack's girlfriend. We'd been dating for over a week. I relaxed against Jack's chest. It felt good.

I was grateful that Ethan didn't give any clue as to what had happened between us the night before.

"Did you get me some decent movies?" Jack asked as he nuzzled my ear. I had the unpleasant feeling that he was doing that for Ethan's benefit.

Ethan pulled a stack of videos out of the bag with a flourish. "*Nowhere to Run, Double Impact, Hard Target, Cyborg, Lionheart, Universal Soldier, Timecop.*"

"The Muscles from Brussels!" Jack cried out. "I'm in heaven!" He seemed to totally forget I was there, even though I was still practically sitting on top of him.

"The muscles from Brussels?" I asked, looking from Jack to Ethan and back to Jack. "What are you talking about?"

"Jean-Claude Van Damme," Jack explained. "Greatest kick-boxer in the world. I've seen every one of his movies. He does his own fighting, you know, not like most other actors."

"I even got you *Bloodsport*," Ethan said, holding the video up like a prized possession.

"*Bloodsport*?" I asked, afraid to know what they were talking about now.

"Yes! Yes! Yes!" Jack shrieked excitedly, practically kissing the video box. "Oh, man, this almost makes being stuck at home okay! *Bloodsport* is the absolute best Van Damme movie ever!"

"I also got you some pig-out food," Ethan said, pulling out two bags of cookies and a two-liter bottle of soda. He went to get a glass, then poured some soda for his brother.

As Ethan slipped *Bloodsport* into the VCR, our eyes met, and I felt my cheeks burn bright red. I quickly looked away, afraid that both guys would notice.

Ethan hit the play button on the VCR. "Okay, I'm outta here. See you later."

"Hey, pause it a minute!" Jack ordered. "You know something, Gigi? I don't think you want to be cooped up with me and Jean-Claude all day."

"I don't mind," I said. I could easily imagine spending the day on the couch with Jack, wrapped in his arms—it wouldn't matter what was on the screen.

"Listen, someone on the team gave me two free passes to go ice-skating today," Jack went on.

"But you can't skate," I said. "You can barely walk."

"I know, but Ethan—"

"I'd be happy to," Ethan said, looking directly at me.

"Hey, that was easy." Jack looked pleased with himself. "I'll see you guys in a couple of hours."

Ethan was already out the door, probably to get his skates. "Excuse me, but isn't anyone going to ask me what I want to do?" I asked, a bit too harshly.

"I'm sorry," Jack apologized, looking truly repentant. "I just assumed you'd rather go ice-skating than watch the movie. But if you'd rather stay here with me, that's even better."

Jack moved closer to me, our lips practically touching now. "Yeow!" Jack jumped up as if he'd just been bitten by something.

"Oh, no!" I cried. I leaped out of the way as I felt freezing-cold liquid seep onto my jeans.

We were soaked with soda, the half-empty bottle flat on its side in the middle of the couch.

Ethan flung open the door. "What happened? Did you bang your ankle?"

"No," Jack said angrily, picking up the soda bottle and placing it on the floor.

Ethan stared at my wet jeans, then at his fuming brother. "I'm sorry, Jack. I must have forgotten to put the cap back on the bottle," he said. He seemed to be holding back a smile.

"If I didn't know you better, I'd say you did that on purpose," Jack growled, holding his leg away from the puddle on the couch.

"Why would I purposely leave the cap off the soda bottle?"

"I can think of a reason or two."

"That's insane."

"Is it?"

"Yeah," Ethan said.

Jack and Ethan stared at each other. Finally Jack turned his head and looked at me. We both knew the moment was over; the romance was lost. It's hard to get back in a romantic mood when you're covered with cold, sticky soda.

"Just go, all right? Go skating. The maid will clean all this up."

Ethan led me out the door and told me he'd meet me downstairs in the courtyard. "I'll just be a minute. Why don't you go home and change your jeans while you're waiting? They look soaked. And don't forget your skates."

"Have fun, Gigi. I'll see you later," Jack called after me as I escaped down the stairs.

*What am I going to do now?* I wondered. Spending an entire day alone with Ethan was not a smart move. Especially since I couldn't stop thinking about the night before. Couldn't stop feeling Ethan's lips touching mine.

Couldn't stop wishing it would happen again . . .

# Chapter Seven

"**H**EY, I'VE GOT a great idea," Ethan said as we skated around the ice for about the hundredth time.

"What?"

"How about two apple ciders and a seat by the heater?" he asked as he guided us toward the refreshment stand.

We'd spent the last hour or so trying to steer clear of wild little boys speeding along with their hockey gear in tow, girls in pretty skating outfits twirling in the center of the ice, and moms and dads trying to keep their toddlers upright.

We ordered the ciders and made our way to the balcony overlooking the rink. We found a spot out of the way of nervous parents keeping an eye on their kids.

We sat in silence, and my eyes drifted to

couple after couple skating together. Most were arm in arm—if they could keep their balance—laughing and occasionally trying to kiss (although that seemed pretty hard to do while ice-skating).

I imagined me and Jack skating together. I shivered as I dreamed of his arms around me.

"Are you cold?" Ethan asked.

"No," I answered. For some reason I felt self-conscious about mentioning Jack to Ethan, especially since they had almost gotten into a fight before.

Ethan and I sat in comfortable silence for a few minutes. My thoughts drifted between Jack and Ethan, comparing the brothers, comparing my feelings for each of them. It was as if somehow the wires had been crossed. I loved Jack, yet Ethan's kiss had been more powerful, even though he was just a friend.

I remembered the last time Ethan and I had skated together. It had been Ethan's twelfth birthday, and Mrs. Chandler had brought a bunch of us kids to the ice rink. Ethan and I had pretended we were ice dancers in the Olympics. Jack had been off playing tag with some of his buddies.

Suddenly something Jack had said about Ethan popped into my mind. Had Ethan ever gone out on a date? Or was he really not interested in falling in love, as Jack had hinted? I felt this sudden, overwhelming urge to find out.

"Have you ever been in love?" I asked Ethan abruptly.

He took a moment before answering. "I . . . uh, thought I was."

"Really?" I felt a tiny stab of jealousy. Ethan Chandler, the loner, the long-distance runner, had been in love. I had to know more. "Who was she? How come I never knew about this? Why didn't you ever tell me about her?" I demanded all at once.

He shook his head. "It doesn't matter now."

"Why not?"

He shrugged. "Nothing ever happened. She never felt the same way. She liked me and all, but she never took me seriously. She looked right through me. As if I weren't there."

"That must have hurt. That was exactly the way it was with Jack and me before I went to Paris. Hey, maybe you should go away like I did."

"I don't think that would make much of a difference." He took another gulp of his cider.

"I still can't believe I never knew you were in love. I know a few girls who've had crushes on you, but you never seemed interested in them."

"You thought I was just a chemistry club kind of guy who runs long distances. A nerd. A geek," he said, sounding strangely bitter. "I'm only interested in achieving things, not in having relationships. Isn't that it, Gigi?"

"I never thought that about you," I protested. "How could I? I know you're not a geek or a nerd. You just surprised me, that's all. I never thought you were interested in anyone before."

He downed the last of his cider, crumpled the plastic cup, and moved back toward the ice.

Subject closed.

The ice wasn't just on the rink. It had definitely become icy between us.

I finished my cider quickly and followed him out onto the ice. At first I thought he might stay angry at me for being so nosy, but after a few stiff minutes he loosened up, and we started having fun again. We ended up playing tag with a group of little boys who were wearing hockey jerseys and helmets.

When the loudspeaker announced that the public skate was over, I didn't want our day to end.

"Do you want to go to Espresso Pacifico?" Ethan suggested as we made our final tour of the ice.

Espresso Pacifico was a café that had the best hot chocolate in Winnetka.

"That's a great idea," I agreed. "Race you to the exit!" I called as I got a good head start.

"Mmmm," I said, taking a whiff of the steaming hot chocolate the waitress put down before me. "I forgot how good this place was."

"Yeah. It's become a weakness for me this past year," Ethan said, biting into his chicken sandwich. "But I never had such good company." He looked over at me and smiled.

I leaned back. His skin was glowing from the brisk autumn air. He looked cute in his woolly green sweater and faded old jeans—cuter than I wanted to admit. *You're with Ethan, Gigi,* I told myself. *And he's not your boyfriend. His brother is.*

I took a deep breath. "So tell me. What's been happening in Winnetka?" I asked.

Ethan caught me up on what had happened at school while I was gone. We also talked about the future—where we wanted to go and things we wanted to accomplish.

I wanted to be a journalist, reporting on the most exciting events of the day, all over the world. Ethan wanted to be a chemist, learning about the building blocks of the universe and finding cures for diseases that started inside the genetic code.

And those dreams were just for starters.

I told him about wanting to travel to Asia on a freighter. He said he wanted to climb Mt. Everest. We both wanted to go to Easter Island to see those weird huge stone statues. And we were both determined to move as far away from Winnetka as we could.

"Hey, we close at five on Sundays!" the manager yelled out to us from the kitchen.

Five?

"Oh, no, it can't be that late! I promised Becky I'd rent a movie with her tonight," I said, frantically cleaning up the mess we'd made at the table. "She wants to tell me all about last night with Andrew."

"They turned into a couple overnight, huh?"

"She's liked him for such a long time. And I guess he felt the same way. It was just that neither one of them had the nerve to say anything."

"Nice when things finally work out."

"Yeah, it is, isn't it?"

He nodded. "So, I guess you want to come over? See how Jack's doing?"

Jack . . .

The hours had flown by, and I hadn't thought about Jack since we'd left the ice rink. I'd been too engrossed in my conversation with Ethan. Usually when I was away from Jack for even a few hours, I started to miss him. But that day had been different. I hadn't missed him in the least. And it scared me.

"Uh . . . sure. I'll stop by," I said slowly.

It was as if a magic spell between Ethan and

me had been broken simply by saying Jack's name.

We walked outside to the car. It was just starting to drizzle. I looked up and stuck out my tongue, waiting to taste a cool drop. Ethan did the same.

"Got it," I said as I felt the tiny pinprick of cold.

"Me too."

"What did you wish for?" I asked.

It was an old wives' tale that if you made a wish after tasting a raindrop, your wish would come true.

"Can't tell you," Ethan said, moving toward his Jeep. "If you say your wish, it won't come true."

Ethan didn't even ask what I had wished for. Not that I would have told him.

I kept saying my wish to myself over and over. *I want Jack Chandler to fall in love with me. I want Jack Chandler to fall in love with me. . . .* But somehow I didn't think I meant it. Or did I?

I opened the Jeep's passenger door and slid in next to Ethan. I felt so perplexed about my relationship with Jack. I'd waited a long time for this, I'd nursed a crush from afar for long enough, and now finally things were working out between us. I couldn't let anything get in the way, especially not some minor attraction to his brother.

Ethan was just my friend, I reminded myself for what seemed like the millionth time. That was why it was so easy to be with him.

Ethan was just a friend. . . .

Then why did spending time with him now leave me feeling so confused?

Ethan turned into the Chandlers' private road. He parked by the fountain in front of his house and turned to me. He looked so unhappy as he touched the side of my cheek.

"Gigi, I have to tell you something," he said. "It's about the dance last night. Even though Jack did sprain his ankle, that's not why he didn't pick you up himself. You weren't really his—"

*Boom! Boom! Boom!*

I nearly shrieked as I saw a fist reach around from the passenger's side and pound on the windshield.

It was Jack, wearing clean sweats and a devastating grin. His hair was rumpled, and he looked gorgeous.

*And he's mine,* I thought. *All mine . . .*

Whatever Ethan had been trying to say in his usual roundabout way vanished from my mind as I looked at Jack. How could I ever confuse the friendly feeling I had for Ethan with the passion that Jack inspired in me?

My heart lurched back into normal gear as I rolled down the window. "What are you doing out here?" I asked. "Aren't you supposed to be lying down inside?"

Jack opened the door for me and held out his hand. I took it as I jumped out of the Jeep. He didn't let go even when I was safely on the ground.

"I just said good-bye to the physical therapist," Jack said. "We worked together most of the afternoon. And guess what? He says I'll be up and around in two or three days. I'll have to miss school tomorrow, which is amazingly lucky, because I have a trig midterm I'm not ready for. We should celebrate—the Evanston game is saved! I'll definitely be on my feet by Saturday."

"You're on your feet right now," Ethan pointed out, still sitting in the Jeep.

"You've got a point there." Jack took my other hand in his, and we stood facing each other. "Your cheeks are pink," he said softly. "You look even more beautiful than usual. Did you have a good time at the rink?"

I nodded.

"Yeah, actually, we did," Ethan answered for me.

"Good," Jack said, not taking his eyes from me. I thought he was going to kiss me. But he hesitated and looked at Ethan, who was still standing there.

"Okay, bro, your services as an escort are no longer required," Jack said, slipping his arm around my shoulder. "You can go now."

I flinched. Jack was being so rude to his brother. This was a side of Jack I'd never seen before—and one that I didn't find very attractive. But my life *would* be simpler once Ethan stopped filling in for Jack. My emotions would finally get off this crazy roller coaster.

Without a word, Ethan turned and headed into the house.

"Thanks, Ethan," I called to his back. "Thanks for taking me skating. It was fun."

But he didn't turn around. I watched as his green sweater disappeared.

"I wonder what's eating him?" Jack asked no one in particular. He didn't seem to care about Ethan's feelings.

I thought of saying that perhaps it was his own rudeness that had offended Ethan, but I didn't want to get into a fight with Jack. Not when things were going so well.

"Come on, let's go sit down," Jack said, leading me to the pool terrace. "I should stay off this ankle, anyway."

We ended up sharing a lounge chair. He sat down first and pulled me down after him. I sat between his legs, leaning back against his chest, my legs stretched out, careful to avoid touching his bad foot.

We sat there together for a long minute. He

wrapped his arms around me and kissed the back of my neck. My entire body shuddered with sensation.

Jack must have heard me sigh.

"Are you happy, Gigi?" he asked

I nodded. I'd never felt happier—or more confused—in my life.

# Chapter Eight

JACK WASN'T IN school Monday. He'd asked me to pick up some homework assignments and bring them to him after school.

I was really beginning to feel like his girlfriend. And it was a strange feeling. A feeling that I had waited for, dreamed of, most of my life.

When I arrived at the Chandlers', Jack was lying on the couch—which had been professionally cleaned of every drop of soda—watching one of the movies Ethan had brought him the day before. He was wearing a cotton sweater over jeans. His hair was damp, as if he'd just gotten out of the shower. And it looked as though he'd just shaved.

*He really got all spruced up for me,* I thought with pleasure.

His bare feet—one still wrapped in a bandage—rested on the arm of the sofa.

He muted the movie when I came in. "Hi, Gigi," he said with a smile. "I'm so glad to see you. It's been just me and Jean-Claude all day."

I handed him his assignments and perched on the edge of the sofa. "Sounds like an exciting day."

"Not as exciting as your being here," he said, pulling me to him. He kissed me long and hard. There was nothing tentative about Jack. And this was the most passionate he had ever been with me. Yet somehow I wasn't reacting the way I'd thought I would. His arms were squeezing me a little too tightly, and it was hard to breathe.

I gently pushed against his chest and came up for air.

"So, how's the foot?" I asked.

"Getting better. I did my physical therapy exercises all morning. It's making a big difference."

"Great!" I said. "Because Becky gave me two tickets for the play *Our Town*. The school drama club is putting it on, and Becky is in it. I thought we could go together." This would be a really public date—everyone at school would know for sure we were a couple.

"When did you want to go?" he asked.

"Wednesday night—that's the first performance. Becky really wants all her friends there that night."

"Wednesday? I don't know. I might not even go to school Wednesday. . . ."

I tried to hide my disappointment, but Jack must have seen it in my face.

"This is really important to you, isn't it?"

"Yes, it is," I said.

"Well, in that case . . . ," he began.

*Great! He'll go,* I thought.

"Ethan can take you," he finished.

"Ethan? But Jack, I want to go with you." Once again I felt I was on an emotional roller coaster.

"I thought you liked Ethan, Gigi. He's my brother. He owes me from when we were kids and I kept the bullies from pounding his glasses into his face. Besides, he won't mind taking you."

"Okay," I said reluctantly. "If Ethan's free, I guess he can take me." Jack was whom I wanted to be with. Jack was my boyfriend. So why was a little voice inside my head telling me the real reason I was afraid to go with Ethan was that Ethan made me feel things I didn't want to feel with anyone except Jack?

"Oh, he'll be free," Jack assured me. "What else could he possibly have to do?" He hit the mute button, and the sound from the TV blasted the room. "What time should I tell him to pick you up?"

★　　★　　★

On Tuesday I was standing by my locker between second and third periods when Becky caught up with me. I'd expected her to give me a progress report on her budding relationship with Andrew Barnes, but she had something else on her mind.

"You will not believe what I just heard," she said.

Before I even had a chance to guess, she blurted out, "Ethan's going out with Lydia Joyner."

The warning bell had sounded. Two minutes to get to chemistry. I yanked the books I needed out of my locker and slammed it shut.

"What?" I said, shocked. I couldn't believe my ears.

"He's going to meet her tonight at Espresso Pacifico at seven."

I swallowed. That was where he had taken me. "How do you know?" I asked, trying to sound casual.

"Lydia was talking to Karen Haupt in study hall. I was sitting at the table next to theirs. I couldn't hear everything they said, but I still got a lot of their conversation. She said that Jack hadn't been returning her phone calls. And then she said something about Jack and the dance on Saturday that didn't make much sense, since you were Jack's date for the dance, not her. Then she said that she was meeting Ethan at Espresso

Pacifico. I guess she's finally giving up on Jack and making her move for the next in line for the Chandler fortune. Anyway, I think Ethan's making a huge mistake by taking her out," Becky finished.

"Why? It's a free country. And, of course, Lydia is gorgeous. If Ethan wants to pick up Jack's leftovers, that's his business," I said with more malice than I realized I had been feeling.

"You're really worked up over this. What gives? I'd think you'd be glad Lydia's throwing in the towel. At least she won't be hanging all over Jack anymore, shoving her cleavage in his face," Becky said.

"I don't know—it's nothing. I guess I just expected Ethan to confide in me," I said slowly. "I mean, I used to tell him all about how I felt—mostly about Jack. I wonder why he didn't mention he was going to ask Lydia out? We spent most of Sunday afternoon together. It's not as if he didn't have a chance to say anything."

"Maybe he didn't think it was important," Becky suggested. I could tell she was trying to make me feel better. We both knew that a date with Lydia Joyner was big news.

Other students surged around us, then seemed to evaporate as the final bell rang.

Becky looked around the empty hall. "Look, I have to run. I'm supposed to be in gym climbing ropes today. I hear Coach Henderson lights a match at the bottom if you don't climb fast enough—there are still kids stuck to the ceiling."

"Catch up with you at lunch?" I asked.

"Sure," she said. "Usual table."

Becky took off, and I was left alone with my thoughts.

But my thoughts weren't very good company.

As I walked slowly toward the chemistry lab, I thought about Ethan having a hot chocolate with Lydia at Espresso Pacifico. Would they sit side by side at the window booth and watch the people pass? Or opposite each other, so they could hold hands across the table? Would they laugh together? Would they share their secrets and dreams? Would he kiss her . . . like he had kissed me? Would we all end up double-dating?

Then a voice interrupted my thoughts. "Miss Pelka, I'm so delighted you have decided to grace us with your presence."

I looked up at the open door to the classroom and saw Dr. Morgan in her rumpled lab coat. She peered over her red-framed glasses. Beyond her were my classmates, some of them giggling, all of them staring.

"I'm not jealous," I said firmly, marching into the room and continuing the conversation I had been having in my mind.

"Excuse me?" Dr. Morgan asked.

"Oh," I said, looking around the room. "I just said I'm sorry I'm late."

"Apology accepted. Now get moving. We're doing several important experiments today, and we have a tight schedule."

I hustled past her and took a seat at the farthest lab table. Raymonda Dabaday was sitting next to me, and she handed me a pair of goggles.

"Thanks," I whispered, pulling the goggles onto my face.

"No problem. You look like you have a lot on your mind."

"Sure do."

For the next half hour, Raymonda basically did our experiment for us—holding a pinch of magnesium over a Bunsen burner. As the sparks began to crackle, she wrote down the results in her lab notebook and let me copy them.

I couldn't keep my mind on what we were supposed to be doing. I couldn't stop thinking about Ethan and Lydia and their date. But how could I feel jealous? Ethan was just a friend. Still, I couldn't get his kiss out of my mind.

And Lydia, of all people! She was my archrival for Jack's affections. She never made it much of a secret that she thought I didn't belong in Winnetka at all—Winnetka was for beautiful, rich people like her . . . and Jack.

Back and forth. Back and forth. Jealousy and anger. I was driving myself crazy!

I kept wanting to ask Ethan, "Why? Why are

you going out with Lydia?" But I knew it wasn't my place to ask.

I wanted to take Lydia's long blond hair and twist it around her pretty neck . . . well, maybe that was a little drastic. But I definitely wanted to make her squirm.

Then I realized Lydia wasn't to blame for anything. It didn't make sense to be mad at her. She hadn't done anything wrong. She was just going out with an unattached guy who'd asked her.

"How about if I do the cleanup?" I suggested to Raymonda, snapping back to attention just as the experiment was ending. I felt sure I could easily handle cleaning up.

Raymonda put her hand on mine. "Forget it," she said kindly. "You're way too messed up. Your mind's not here today. You'd probably end up breaking a beaker and cutting yourself. Just write up our lab conclusion. Okay?"

"Thanks."

Somehow I managed—I'm not sure how—to make it through the rest of chem lab. And I'd never been more grateful for the bell.

"If you don't mind my asking, what's up with you today?" Raymonda asked me as the class piled out of the lab and into the packed hallway.

"Love problems," I admitted.

"Ah, Ethan Chandler, right?" she said.

"Yes—I mean no. I'm going out with his brother, Jack."

She did a double take. "Jack Chandler? Oh, he's cool. So handsome. So funny. So nice. You're a lucky girl."

We stopped at my locker.

"Yeah, I guess I am," I said dejectedly.

"Hope it all works out."

"So do I."

Raymonda waved good-bye.

I opened my locker and shoved all my books inside. Then I took out my lunch bag and slammed the door shut. I walked the entire way to the cafeteria as if I were in a dream.

Becky was already at our table. I threw my lunch on the table and sat beside her.

"You look shell-shocked," she said. "Have you been thinking about Ethan's making the mistake of his life?"

"Yeah, but I think I've got it under control."

"Oh, really?" She didn't sound convinced.

I took a deep breath. "If Ethan and Lydia want to go out, that's their business. I just think it's strange that a guy who's never had a date in his life would pick Lydia. I guess Ethan and Jack have more in common than I thought."

I looked up and saw Andrew Barnes heading for our table.

"Becky, I'm going to eat outside," I said, picking up my lunch bag. "I need to be by myself for a little while. See you later?"

"Okay, sure. Meet you at the flagpole

after school. We'll walk home together."

Just as I made my escape, Andrew slipped into an empty seat at our table. He gave Becky a quick kiss on the mouth. And as they sat together, their heads nearly touching, I realized how perfect they were together.

My love life wasn't even close.

So there I was. Gigi Pelka—chic, sophisticated, fresh from Paris—was sitting on a paper bag and eating a bologna sandwich under the old elm on Winnetka High's front lawn. How had it come to this?

Jack and Ethan. Ethan and Jack. I had never liked anyone but Jack. Not once. Not even in junior high, when my friends would flit from one boy to the next. It had always been Jack. And it always would be Jack . . . or so I'd thought up to now. But being with Jack wasn't quite how I'd imagined it would be. He was definitely cute. Definitely athletic. And most definitely a good kisser. It was nice to be Jack's girlfriend. Nice to be envied by all the girls in my class. But there was something missing. Something wasn't right.

I took a bite of my bologna sandwich. Ethan was a friend. Just a friend. But when Becky had told me about his date with Lydia, I felt sick to my stomach. I didn't want him going out with Lydia. I didn't want him going out with anyone—anyone, I realized, but me. But it was too late.

"So let me get this straight," Becky began. She'd been sitting on her bed, concentrating on her pedicure. Now she looked at me as if she didn't speak the same language I did. "You waited all day to tell me that after seven years of nursing the most outstanding lust in history, the most amazing infatuation of the century, that when you kiss Jack Chandler, you feel nothing?"

"Pretty much nothing," I admitted dismally.

"Zero? Zip? *Nada?* But when you kissed Ethan, you felt the earth move?"

"Oh, Becky, I felt everything. Out there on the track, when I should have been with Jack, I kissed Ethan and felt . . ." I couldn't think of the words, and gestured feebly.

"Stars in the sky?"

"Yeah."

"Was your heart galloping like a racehorse? Were you unable to catch your breath? Did you wish it could go on and on?"

"Yeah, yeah, and yeah," I moaned. "I've really messed up this time, Becky. I feel so horrible and wonderful and giddy and stupid all at the same time."

"C'mon, you haven't totally messed up. It's simple, actually. You're in love with Ethan. Not Jack. Get it straight."

"But I can't be! I know I'm in love with Jack. I've always been in love with Jack. I've thought about him, dreamed about him, hugged my pillow and pretended it was him . . ." I got up and started pacing from one end of her room to the other.

"Why can't you just face the truth? There's no doubt you're in love with Ethan—or at least in extreme like. Why don't you give him a chance for once?"

"Because I've wanted Jack Chandler my whole life, and now I finally have him. I can't just walk away from my one chance at happiness with Jack."

"Listen, Jack is just a crush that got out of control—*way* out of control." Becky waved the nail polish brush in my face. "Every girl in Winnetka has had a crush on him at least once in her life. And why not? Jack's a total hunk. And now you've got him. But I'm not sure it was, is, or ever will be love."

"Then what was it? I mean, what *is* it?" I corrected myself.

"I don't know. But this thing with Ethan could be for real. Maybe even true love. Why don't you just go on over to the Chandlers' house and tell Ethan to ditch Lydia tonight? Tell him how you really feel."

"Get real, Becky. It's not that simple. Besides, I can't go from thinking I've been . . .

whatever . . . with Jack all my life to being in love with Ethan just like that." I snapped my fingers.

"Why not, if that's how you really feel?" she said matter-of-factly.

"What kind of person am I to switch my feelings on and off like that? How can I possibly be that kind of girl?" I was pacing even faster than before.

"Gigi, you've got to stop that. I'm getting dizzy watching you."

I stopped. "Listen, Becky, I can't be in love with Ethan," I said, flopping down on her bed. "I just can't!"

Becky shrieked as I jostled her and she accidentally painted a ruby-red line across her toenail and onto her foot. She grabbed tissues and nail polish remover from the nightstand.

"I'm sorry, Becky. Now I'm even messing up *your* life—or at least your pedicure."

"Don't worry about it. Nobody's going to see my feet anyway, except maybe in gym class. Okay, now answer this question honestly, without any shoulds or woulds or the history of your crush on Jack. Ready?" Becky asked.

"I guess so."

"What's so terrible about falling in love with Ethan?"

"Becky, I . . . I just . . ."

"Just what?"

I took a deep breath. "I don't want to be fickle. I don't want to think of myself that way. I'm not like—"

"Like Jack?" she asked sweetly.

"Come on, he's not that bad."

Becky bent her head forward and appeared to concentrate on wiping the nail polish from her toes. "Well, he was that bad last year. I didn't mention this in my letters because I didn't want to upset you, but Jack Chandler was not exactly a monk while you were away in Paris. I'm not saying he doesn't have true feelings for you now. He might have changed. But then so have you. You're not the same girl who went away last year. You've seen a little bit of the world. Outside of Winnetka, Jack Chandler is just another guy, not the center of the universe. Maybe you've changed enough to be ready for Ethan in a way you weren't before," Becky said, twisting the cap closed on the bottle of nail polish.

My mind was spinning. What would happen if I did go over to the Chandlers' and break things off with Jack? What if I told Ethan I wanted to be more to him than just a friend? What if I said I wanted him to forget about Lydia Joyner and start thinking about dating me? What if . . . what if the earth was suddenly sucked into the sun?

"Earth to Gigi. Earth to Gigi. Come in, Gigi," Becky said, interrupting my thoughts.

"Sorry, Becky. I just zoned out for a minute," I said, shaking my head to clear my thoughts. "There's only one problem with your plan."

"What's that?"

"Ethan doesn't want to go out with me."

"Right, and the moon's made of cheese."

"No, really, Becky. Ethan's only been spending time with me lately because Jack asked him to. I bet he's liked Lydia all along but didn't do anything about it because she and Jack were an item—even if it was an on-and-off kind of relationship. But now that he sees Jack and I are becoming serious, he figures it's okay for him to make his move on Lydia."

"Lydia? He's always made jokes about her."

"Only because of me. He knew how I felt about her. But now he doesn't have to hide his feelings for Lydia. And maybe, just maybe, she feels the same way about him."

"I doubt that Lydia Joyner has ever had a sincere emotion in her life. And I refuse to believe Ethan's been nursing a crush on Lydia all this time."

"Why not? She's beautiful and—"

"And so are you," Becky finished.

"Right," I said with a sigh. "Hey, I think I just figured out why I didn't feel anything when I kissed Jack."

"Oh, yeah? Why?"

"I was too nervous. You know, I haven't

125

kissed many guys in my life. Maybe I just didn't know what to do."

"It was your first time with Ethan, and you did a pretty good job," she argued. She waited for some reaction from me. When I didn't comment, she continued. "All right, Gigi, maybe you're right. Maybe you just need a few more practice kisses with Mr. Wonderful. I kissed Andrew on Saturday night, and it was kind of awkward at first."

"Really? I saw how he looked at you in the cafeteria. So are you two a definite item now?"

"We're taking it slow. I'm not like you, Gigi. I don't feel passionate about everything and everyone. But we did kiss. A few times. And eventually we got the hang of it."

I shrieked with delight. Becky just smiled a wicked smile, as if she'd done some major mischief.

"That's so great!" I said.

"Good. Now get out of here. Andrew's on his way over to do some homework with me."

"Yeah, right—homework. I'll bet you don't get any schoolwork done tonight." I picked up my stuff and headed for the door. "Thanks for telling me about you and Andrew. Maybe I still have a chance for love," I said as I left.

But with whom?

At precisely six-fifty that evening, I watched as Ethan walked out of the house, took a deep breath, and stood next to his Jeep for a long moment.

I spied on Ethan for several minutes. He seemed to be enjoying the crisp autumn air. Was he looking forward to the night ahead of him? His night with Lydia Joyner?

He brushed his hair back from his forehead several times and bit his lower lip. I recognized that habit of his.

"Nerves," I said aloud. "We're both nervous." Ethan was finally going on a date with the love of his life. I should have felt happy for him—he was coming out of his shell.

Besides, I had a date with the love of my life that night, too.

So why did I feel so miserable?

# Chapter Nine

I TORE MYSELF away from the window as Ethan drove away. I had been staring out the window for so long, I hadn't left myself much time to get dressed. I put on the navy blue vest dress I'd bought with Véronique, quickly braided my hair, and grabbed a cotton sweater. I tugged on my cowboy boots as I headed out of my room.

"Bye, Dad," I yelled as I walked to the front door.

"Mmph," he grunted without lifting his head from his computer keyboard.

I walked the short distance across the courtyard and let myself in the Chandlers' kitchen door—I knew that Mr. and Mrs. Chandler were out for dinner, and the maid didn't work on Tuesdays.

"Hey, Gigi!" Jack called out from the study.

I followed his voice and found him sitting in a brown leather armchair. A tray of chips and sodas was laid out in front of him. A toasty fire blazed in the fireplace, and the wide-screen TV was on.

"Hi," I said, sitting down next to him. "Whatcha watching?"

"The tape of our last game," he said, barely taking his eyes from the screen. "I'm going over the second-quarter plays."

"Why?" I asked, looking at Jack leaping high into the air to avoid a tackle.

Jack paused the tape and turned to me.

"Even though we eventually won the game, we lost ground in the second quarter," he explained patiently. "I was studying the plays to see where we went wrong. The local cable company tapes all our games, and I made a deal with them to mail me a copy each week."

"And then you watch yourself for hours?"

"C'mon, Gigi, it's not an ego thing. Really. It's my job. I want to be the best quarterback I can be. There's a lot more involved than you think. I have to study the other team, all the great plays of other games. I need to learn from my mistakes. Being the starting quarterback isn't just doing a few push-ups during practice and then getting out there on the field, throwing the ball, and hoping somebody catches it."

"I guess I never thought about it before."

Jack was serious about playing football. He wasn't just some dumb jock who wanted to get out there and bang heads. He was into the strategy of the game. The thinking aspect of it. I admired that.

"So that's my homework for tonight, watching the second quarter."

"I could run home and get my math," I joked. "We could do our homework together—you'll watch television, and I'll hit the books."

He shook his head. "No way. Homework's for later. Now that I've got you here, I've got only one thing on my mind," he said, running his hand up my arm. When he reached my shoulder, he pulled me to him.

"What's that?" I asked, as if I didn't know.

"This," he said as his lips touched mine.

I closed my eyes, but instead of picturing Jack, an image of Ethan filled my mind.

Ethan . . .

As Jack kissed me I thought about what Becky had said. Had my crush for Jack gotten out of control? Had it prevented me from seeing the truth? Was it possible that I really was in love with Ethan?

Ethan . . . who was at that very moment on his date with Lydia at Espresso Pacifico.

Without my realizing it, Jack's lips had left mine. He was looking longingly at the television set. But I wasn't in the least offended. Actually, I was relieved.

"Hey, Jack, how about if we watch that second quarter?" I suggested. "You can show me all the important parts."

"I've got a better idea—how about I show you the third quarter? That's when we really picked up some steam," Jack said enthusiastically. He quickly grabbed the remote control and pushed fast forward.

In seconds we were watching Jack run across the wide-screen TV, and between mouthfuls of snacks and soda he told me all about each move and play. I wasn't at all surprised to find that Jack was the hero of every single one. And as he continued to praise himself, to tell me how brilliant he'd been, how strong, how fast, and how determined he was, I began to wonder whether Jack really was my dream guy after all.

At that moment Jack seemed like an insecure, self-centered jock who needed to be constantly reassured that he was the very best.

At everything.

I guzzled the last drops of soda in my glass and noticed the time on the antique grandfather clock in the corner. Ten-thirty. I had to get out of there before Ethan came home from his date with Lydia. My feelings for Jack were changing too fast. I needed time to think things through. Time alone, without either of the Chandler brothers.

"Well, I guess I'll be going," I said, getting up from the couch.

"Wait, you've gotta see this play," Jack said, pointing to the big screen. "It's the best. I totally saved the team from—"

"Sorry, Jack, I really have to go," I said firmly.

"But you're going to miss the absolute best part! The final two minutes are unbelievable. We're two yards from a touchdown, and the other team is going for a blitz. Just as I'm about to be sacked—"

"Some other time, okay?" I interrupted, moving toward the door. "I've got a lot of homework."

"So bring it over here. I'll mute this so you can work."

I shook my head. It was obvious that Jack didn't want to be left alone, and before that night, I couldn't have imagined not wanting to be alone with him.

I wished I could tell him the truth—that my feelings for him were changing, changing against my will. I was doubting that what I felt for him was true love. But I couldn't tell him that, and I certainly couldn't tell him the real reason I didn't want to stay any longer—that I didn't want to run into Ethan, because I thought I was falling in love with him.

But there was one thing I was absolutely sure of—I had to get out of the Chandler house before Ethan got home. What if he had brought

Lydia back to the house? What if they were dancing on the pool terrace when I left? What if I interrupted their kiss the way Ethan had interrupted mine and Jack's?

I was almost out the door when I saw Jack's pitiful expression. "I'm sorry, Jack. I know it stinks being cooped up here all day."

"Yeah. It's the worst," he said, munching on a chip.

"But I can't do intense math assignments with other people around me," I said, sticking with my earlier excuse and hoping it would get me out of there without hurting Jack's feelings. "And trig is totally intense."

"But you were going to bring it over earlier. Why not now?" he asked. "It's too late for me to call anyone else."

"I really have to go," I said. Now I was getting annoyed.

"Oh, okay," he said, grabbing hold of my hand. "I'll let you go after one last kiss." He pulled me to him with such force that I ended up on top of him in the leather chair. One hand held my waist, and the other pressed my head down to meet his face.

"Jack, stop, you're hurting—"

And that's when Ethan walked in.

I quickly pulled away from Jack.

"So, how was Lydia?" Jack asked, adjusting himself on the leather chair.

Ethan shrugged. "Okay."

"I've got to go home. Finish my homework," I said, standing up with as much dignity as I could muster and moving toward the door again.

"I'll get your jacket," Ethan said, following me.

"I didn't bring one." Why did Ethan feel he always had to take care of me? I wished he'd just leave me alone. He had Lydia now.

"Do you want to borrow mine?" he asked.

"No, thanks."

"It's chilly out there," he persisted.

"I'm just going across the courtyard," I said. "I think I can handle it without your jacket."

"Hey, what's going on with you two? Why are you snapping at each other?" Jack said.

"I'm not snapping," I snapped. "I just don't want his jacket."

"Fine," Ethan said, his face turning an angry red.

"Good," Jack said, unaware of the biting glares Ethan and I continued to exchange. "'Cause don't forget, Ethan's taking you to the play tomorrow night, right?"

*Oh, great,* I thought. *This is just what I need—more time with Ethan. As if my life isn't complicated enough already.*

# Chapter Ten

"**P**LEASE, DAD. YOU just have to let me go back to France," I pleaded the next evening.

I had done some serious, if somewhat frantic, soul-searching that day. And now, less than forty-five minutes before Ethan would pick me up to go see Becky in the school play, I'd finally found the solution to all my troubles.

"But, Gerolyn, you just got home," my dad said, saving the document he was working on at his computer and looking up at me. "And I missed you so much last year."

"I missed you, too, Dad."

"Then why do you want to go back so soon?"

How could I tell him the truth? That I was afraid I was in love with my boyfriend's brother?

I shrugged. "I don't know. I think it would be

good for me. I'd strengthen my language skills even more and deepen my appreciation for European culture."

"That reasoning got you one year away. It doesn't get you a second one. Besides, it's the middle of September. The school year has already begun. And it would be impossible to get an application for a junior year abroad approved this late."

"I could just go on my own. I don't need a special program. I could go back to the International School. I'm sure I could stay with the Thibaults. I miss them, and Véronique. If it's the money, maybe I can get a grant or a scholarship."

"It's not the money, sweetheart. It's the principle. You just got home. I think you just need a little more time to adjust. I know Winnetka can't compare to Paris, but I want you to give it a chance before you run back to France."

"What about England, then? I already know the language. Maybe you could call up one of your colleagues in an environmental group over there and get me an internship. I'm very interested in the environment." I was afraid I sounded as desperate as I felt.

"Gerolyn, what's going on?"

"Dad, I'm miserable here!" I cried. "If you won't let me go away, I think we should at least consider moving. It's time we had a real home, not just a house behind someone else's. This carriage house used to be the Chandler family's horse stables! Don't we deserve something better?"

He looked away, stung by my words.

I knew I'd hit a sore spot. My dad loved our house. It held the memory of my mother, dead now for more than a decade.

"Dad, I'm sorry. I didn't mean to upset you." I plopped down in our old rocking chair.

He took off his glasses and wiped them with a tissue. "Come on, Gerolyn, what's really going on here? You looked ecstatic when you came home from the dance on Saturday. And Sunday you were practically glowing after skating with Ethan. I can't figure you out. Was there some boy in France who broke your heart?"

"No," I said. "Nobody in France."

"Is there somebody back here giving you trouble?"

"No," I lied. "Well . . . maybe. Actually, yes."

"Is it Ethan?" His eyes narrowed.

There was no doubt in my mind that if Ethan had walked in the door at that moment, he would have been in major trouble with my dad.

"A little," I said. "But it's not just him."

"And he's why you want to move?"

"Yeah. Him and Jack. And my mixed–up feelings."

"Well, running away from your feelings never works. You have to confront emotions, deal with them. And deal with the people involved."

*Oh, no,* I thought, *here comes the lecture.*

*Now I'll never be ready in time to go to the play with Ethan.*

"Honey, don't you know that if you have a problem, leaving is not the solution? Dealing with it is." My dad always lapsed into psychobabble when it came to emotions.

"I know that, Dad," I said. I was about to give up and figure out how I could save enough money to buy my own plane ticket when Dad took my hand.

"Listen, honey, you can go to France if you're that determined."

I couldn't believe it. I could really go! It took every bit of self-discipline I had not to leap into the air with a victory yell.

"Thanks, Dad. You're the best—"

"In January," he added.

*January?* My shoulders slumped.

"But Dad! Why can't I go now?"

"You have to finish the semester here first. Besides, I figure whatever problem you've got, you'll solve it by January. And then you can go to France, England, the New Hebrides, anywhere you want—but you'll be going because you want to go. Not because you're running away from something." He turned back to his computer and resumed working on his document.

I bit my lip.

"January or not at all," was the last thing he said.

"Okay, Dad, January it is."

There was only one problem with that plan. January was a lifetime away.

Dear Véronique,

I know you're probably really busy, but please, please write and tell me what to do.

Remember Ethan? Well, I think I'm in love with him.

I can't believe that I finally got Jack Chandler, and now I wish I were going out with his brother, Ethan, instead. But Ethan is dating Jack's ex-girlfriend Lydia.

I still like Jack. I still think he's gorgeous and everything. But he's not the perfect guy I thought he was when I was in Paris. In fact, he's far from perfect. He's self-centered, he's insecure, he needs an audience to feel good about himself . . . I could go on and on, believe me.

Should I continue going out with Jack anyway? Maybe this is just a phase and next week I'll realize I am still madly in love with him.

Has that ever happened to you? That you just fall in and out of love like that?

Write soon! I'm desperate!

Love,
Gigi

I still had a few minutes before Ethan was supposed to pick me up and take me to the play. I still had time to get out of it. I picked up the phone and punched in Ethan's number. A moment later I heard Ethan's voice.

"Hi, Ethan. Listen, I'm really sorry, but I can't go with you to the school play tonight," I said into the telephone. I had considered telling him I was sick, but I was afraid he'd come over with a bowl of soup and a box of cough drops.

"How come?"

"I just don't want to," I said. "Isn't that enough of a reason?"

"Is this about Jack?"

"Yes, it's about Jack. At least, it's partly about him. And partly about me . . . and you. I'm not making any sense, am I?"

I wished Ethan would say something, anything, instead of leaving me to babble into the phone like a raving lunatic. But he was silent. I heard only his soft breathing. I remembered the last time I'd heard that sound so close to my ear. . . .

An image of us kissing passionately outside the school that Saturday night flashed into my mind. My body relived the sensations that had flooded me when Ethan's lips touched mine.

I tried to keep the tremor out of my voice. "I

just don't feel right about seeing you. It's too complicated to explain over the phone, but I don't want to explain this in person, either." I knew that if I saw him, I'd end up in his arms . . . the same arms that had probably been wrapped around Lydia Joyner at Espresso Pacifico the night before.

"But what about Becky? She'll be very disappointed if you don't go."

"I'll go another night. There are four performances through the weekend. Becky will understand if I miss one."

"If Jack's ankle were better, he'd take you—"

"Don't tell me what Jack would do!" I said angrily.

Silence.

"Okay," Ethan finally said. "Why don't you tell me the real reason you don't want to see me tonight?"

I moved over to the bay window in my room and shoved aside the collection of stuffed animals my dad had bought me over the years. I sat down, closed my eyes, and felt the tears squeeze out onto my cheeks.

How could I tell him I didn't want to see him because I was falling in love with him, and he was with someone else now?

"Ethan, I don't want to get into this now. Can't you just drop it?"

I leaned my face against the cool pane of glass,

opened my eyes again, and couldn't believe what I saw.

"Ethan, what are you doing?" I demanded.

I looked out the window and directly into his face—on the other side of my window! Ethan's brown eyes stared into mine. In his hand was his portable phone.

"I just jumped onto the gate outside your kitchen door, climbed the gutter to the roof of the porch, then swung up to the ledge," he said. "It's not as easy as it was when I was twelve years old—remember when I tried to fool you into thinking it was snowing in July by sprinkling powder on your window? At any rate, getting up here was close to impossible with a phone in my hand. So are you going to make me stand out here on the ledge all night?" he asked into the phone.

"Oh . . . no, come on in," I said, hanging up my extension. I opened the window, and he hopped inside.

"Thanks," he said, turning off his portable phone.

"Ethan, why are you making this so difficult?" I asked, sitting at my desk chair—the safest seat in my room. If I sat anyplace else, he'd probably sit right next to me, and then I'd never be able to do what I had to do, say what I had to say: that I didn't want him to take me out because Jack pressured him to. Because he felt sorry for me.

"I just wanted to talk you out of skipping the play," Ethan said, walking toward me. "We'll have fun—I promise."

"I'm going back to France," I blurted out. "My dad says I can spend another year there. I'm leaving in January."

"Wow!" Ethan sat on my bed, looking shocked. "What made you decide to do that? I thought you and Jack—"

"Forget about me and Jack. He's using you. You need to live your own life. Go out with Lydia. Have fun," I said, looking at the floor.

"Oh, Gigi." Ethan sighed. "I have a confession to make," he said, taking a deep breath. "It's true, Jack's been using me, but that's not the real reason I agreed to take you out."

My stomach clenched.

"I know how you feel about Jack," Ethan began, "how you've always felt about him. But I've been taking advantage of Jack's sprained ankle to spend time with you. To show you."

"Show me?" Could this be true? Was Ethan feeling the same thing I was? Did he want to show me how much he cared?

"I've taken advantage of everything that's happened. I should have driven you right back to our house after Jack got hurt at the dance. I shouldn't have danced with you. I shouldn't have kept you out late at the Depot. I should have remembered to put the cap back on the soda bottle.

"I have no idea whether Jack would've brought you flowers for the dance. He's never done it for any of his other girlfriends. And I don't know if he would have done it for you."

I felt a sudden stab of pain as I finally realized Ethan hadn't wanted to dance with me, spend time with me, or kiss me because he cared for me. No, it wasn't me at all. He'd just wanted to prove his point—that his brother was a loser.

"You wasted your entire weekend to prove to me that Jack is a jerk? That I could have been just as happy with any other guy in the world?"

"No, Gigi. It's that Jack could be happy with any other girl," Ethan whispered.

"Well, you've got it wrong, then. Jack and I care about each other," I said with a chilling certainty—even though I didn't feel that way anymore. "It's as simple as that. And no one can get in the way of that. I can't believe you betrayed your own brother. Not to mention me. I thought we were friends."

"All right. Let's talk about betrayal. Here, look out your window. Can you see into the study?" He squinted as he looked out the window and pointed to the room in his house. "What do you see?"

I could just barely make out two forms on the couch watching TV. One was obviously Jack.

He had his foot up on a stool, and his arm around . . . Karen Haupt. As I watched I saw him pull her to him—like he pulled me to him—and kiss her. They were still kissing when my eyes became too tear-filled to see.

Ethan put his hand on my shoulder. "It's not that Jack is consciously cheating on you. He just doesn't have any clue what it means to care about somebody and think about their feelings first, above and beyond his own," he said evenly.

"Karen Haupt?" I swallowed hard.

"I tried to tell you about Jack. About how he treats girls. But you wouldn't listen to me."

"Is that what you were trying to tell me when you kissed me?" I was so angry with Jack and humiliated by Ethan, I could have strangled them both. "Were you trying to show me how easy it was for a boy to kiss a girl without caring for her? I think that's really low! How could you let me think you were such a great friend? Why didn't you just mind your own business?"

"Because I didn't want to see you get hurt. And because—"

"I'm a big girl!" I burst out. "I can take care of myself. I don't get hurt, except by major manipulators like you." I stood up and paced, too angry to sit in one spot.

"You think I'm the one who'll hurt you? Well, pay attention to this. Jack will love you desperately, seriously, forever—for about two weeks. Then he'll meet another girl and feel that way about her. And you'll feel terrible because your feelings for him will have grown deeper. I know I did some unforgivable things this weekend, but I only did them to protect you. And I'm not sorry I did them, either."

"So you did all this just to protect me?"

"Yeah."

"Well, I don't need your protection. Get out!" I screamed as I tore open the window and flung his portable phone out. It clunked along the porch roof, then fell onto the cobblestone path.

We stared at each other for a long, mind-numbing minute.

"I'll walk downstairs," he said quietly.

"No, I don't want you in my house for another second. Go out the way you came in," I demanded.

He looked as if he might try to talk me out of it, but he must have known he wouldn't win. He slowly stood up and walked to the window. But he stopped in front of me. He was as close as he'd been right before that amazing kiss Saturday night at the dance.

But this time there was no tenderness. Just anger.

I flinched under his gaze, staring at those brown eyes. I couldn't help myself or the way he made me feel deep, deep inside. I was so confused. On the one hand, I was furious at him. On the other, I couldn't help thinking he'd done me a favor—making me see Jack for who he really was.

"What you said . . . you did all that for me?" I choked out.

We continued to stare at each other, but he was the first to turn away.

"No," he said at last, turning toward the window. "It could have been anyone. I just didn't want to see Jack hurt another girl. It had nothing to do with you." And with that he crawled out of the window.

I slammed it shut and heaved a huge, terrible sigh.

That was when I heard Ethan roll down the porch roof and land on the cobblestone path with a thump.

# Chapter Eleven

"WHAT DO YOU think the odds are of two brothers messing up their ankles within a week?" Jack asked me as we walked in front of the Chandler mansion. "Ethan's even worse off than I am. I don't even have to miss one football game. He's going to miss out on the Chicago Marathon and the Winnetka Cancer Drive ten-kilometer run. Plus he might have ruined his chance to make the state championship."

"That's too bad," I said coldly. I imagined Ethan stuck in bed all week. Would Lydia be there, tending to his every need? Probably, as soon as she found out.

"And while we're on that subject," Jack continued, "just what was he doing on your porch roof, anyhow?"

I took a deep breath.

I'd had some time to prepare an answer to that question—I knew Jack would eventually ask it once the excitement of rushing Ethan to the emergency room wore off, after the Chandler family had settled Ethan comfortably in his room, and after Jack had asked me if I'd go for a walk with him.

We'd barely been alone for two minutes, and now he'd jumped right in and asked that dreaded question.

"The same thing you were doing watching TV with Karen Haupt earlier this evening," I countered, although I wasn't as interested in his response as I thought I'd be. I was just stalling for time. The last time I had seen Jack, I'd wondered if I was in love with him anymore. Did I still feel that way now?

"C'mon, she's just a friend," Jack said easily. "You're not jealous, are you?"

"Do you kiss all your friends like that?" I asked sweetly. "What a good friend you are."

"So you were watching me from your window." Jack laughed. "I thought so. I just kissed Karen to make you jealous. To liven up our relationship a bit. The past few days you haven't seemed as, well, eager to see me. I thought maybe you were getting bored with me." He ran his fingers down my back.

"Or maybe you were getting bored with me," I said.

"Oh, Gigi," he said, turning to face me. "I could never get bored with you. Not even after several lifetimes together."

He sounded so sincere. I wished I could believe him. I wished he would kiss me, and every care I'd ever had in my life would fall away as his lips caressed mine. But I knew that could never happen.

Not now.

Not since Ethan had opened my eyes.

"I shouldn't have tried to make you jealous," Jack apologized.

"I'm not jealous," I said truthfully. And I really wasn't. Not one bit.

A wonderful feeling of lightness overcame me as I was finally free from jealousy, totally free from my crush on Jack.

It was over. Definitely over.

And I was one hundred percent relieved.

I didn't love Jack Chandler. I had only loved the idea of Jack. I'd loved the thought of having a handsome, smart, sophisticated guy interested in me. I'd loved the idea of being in love.

But the real Jack Chandler couldn't commit himself to anybody. Ethan had tried to show me that. And even though I still wasn't speaking to him, I had to admit that Ethan was right.

"Well, as long as you're not jealous, why don't you show me? You know what they say— actions speak louder than words," he said as he wrapped his arms around me. Our lips touched, and my decision to break up with Jack was confirmed.

I felt nothing.

As Becky would say: Zero. Zip. *Nada.*

Jack pulled away and looked at me suspiciously. "You know, Gigi, I've dated more than a few girls. And I've broken up with most of them," he began. "So I consider myself an expert on the subject of good-byes. And that kiss tasted an awful lot like good-bye. What's up?"

"Well . . ." I looked down. I hoped I could say what needed to be said. "I've had an amazing crush on you all my life, but now—I don't know why—I just don't feel that way anymore."

He seemed to be thinking about what I'd just said—about how this turn of events would affect his life, whether people would know I had broken up with him. Knowing Jack as I did now, I wouldn't have been surprised if he started a rumor that he had dumped me.

That would be just like Jack—the real Jack Chandler, self-centered, selfish, arrogant, insensitive, insecure . . .

He was so insecure, he needed to be constantly reassured by me—by everyone—that he was great. That was why he needed a parade of girls, because one girl couldn't do the trick by herself, couldn't convince him to believe in himself.

Except maybe someone very special.

Someone with a lot more patience than I had.

"You know, Karen Haupt is really nice," I added. "Maybe you should start dating her."

He nodded.

"You're right. Karen is really nice, and pretty. I never noticed her before because we grew up together—kind of like us, I guess."

"You should give her a call."

"Maybe I will. So . . . can we still be friends?" he asked, holding his hand out.

"Sure," I said, taking his hand in mine.

"By the way, this doesn't have anything to do with Ethan, does it?"

I'd hoped he wouldn't ask that.

"No," I lied, "it has nothing to do with Ethan."

"Good. Then let's go upstairs and cheer him up. I owe him some videos and pig-out food."

I didn't want to go. The last person I wanted to see just then was Ethan Chandler. I felt like such a fool. Here I had thought Ethan liked me as a friend, maybe as more than a friend, and all along he had just been trying to keep another girl from falling for Jack. He had just been trying to protect me from Jack, as he'd have protected anyone. I wasn't special to him. He didn't care for me the way I now realized I cared for him—as more than a friend.

Much more.

"Come on," Jack urged, taking my hand. Just a week earlier I would have felt a surge of pleasure from his touch. Now I felt only a hard tug.

But I wasn't going to explain all this to Jack. Jack, who couldn't see past his own feelings to those of other people, even his own brother.

"All right," I said reluctantly as I followed him upstairs.

Ethan looked like a miserable caged animal in his blue sweats, his leg bandaged and elevated by three fluffed pillows. He looked sad and bored . . . and in pain. I fought the urge to run over to him and give him a huge hug.

He wouldn't want me to hug him. He was through trying to save me from myself.

"Hi," he said tentatively, looking directly at me.

"Hi," I said, sitting down on the clothes hamper by the door. I wished I could leave for Paris that very second. I could finish high school there. Then after a brilliant but cloistered four years at the Sorbonne, I'd get a cheap apartment in Montparnasse and build a career as a journalist. In my spare time I'd write books about searing betrayal and love with tragic consequences. And most important, I'd never have to see Ethan Chandler again in my life.

"Gigi and I thought we'd come by and see if you want us to get anything to make your confinement a little easier," Jack said.

"Thanks," Ethan said in a monotone. He never stopped looking at me.

I looked away. I wondered if Lydia was coming over.

"What's your video order?" Jack asked. "And don't forget about the munchies. Do you crave anything special?"

"I thought you were supposed to stay off your feet until you see the doctor tomorrow," Ethan said.

"I've been on my feet ever since I heard you shout like a dying elephant in the courtyard," Jack pointed out. "Remember who carried you to the car? Remember who carried you to and from the parking lot of the hospital? Remember who carried you up the stairs and into your room? Besides, this family can't cope with two injured sons."

"Well, since you're on your feet, you should take Gigi to the play," Ethan said grimly, turning his face to the window. "If you hurry, you'll just make the end of it."

"I don't think Gigi and I will be going together to anything anymore. But maybe I'll give Karen a call."

"What?" Ethan sat up quickly. "Karen who?"

"Karen Haupt," Jack said easily. "Gigi and I are through."

Ethan looked at me. "Do you mind waiting outside for a few minutes?" he asked. "I have a few things I want to talk to Jack about."

"Uh . . . no. I guess not," I said with a shrug, walking out of the room. But before I could even close the door, Ethan started to yell.

"You broke up with Gigi? You are such a loser! She's funny and smart and beautiful, and the feelings she has for you are way deeper than anything anybody's ever felt for you before!" Ethan shouted. He sounded pretty angry.

I pressed my ear up against the door. For such an expensive house, the walls sure were thin.

"Wow, bro, I didn't realize how much you cared. I'm flattered. And you could be right," Jack said calmly. "But this wasn't my call. Gigi broke up with me."

Silence. "Huh?" Ethan said.

"Just what I said. Gigi broke up with me. But I don't want you to spread that around. It might hurt my reputation."

I shook my head in disgust. Typical Jack. On that note I pushed the door open and walked back in. Ethan looked at me.

"Is this stuff true?" he asked.

"What stuff?" I said innocently.

"Come on, Gigi. I know you were listening."

"Yes. It's true," I said, nodding.

"So," Jack said, patting Ethan on the shoulder, "now that we've got that all cleared up, why don't you give me your video order? I'm ready to go."

"I want *Reality Bites* and an Indiana Jones movie," Ethan said woodenly. "The first one.

And I want the biggest bag of chips you can find, chocolate chip cookies, and a large bottle of orange soda."

"You got it, bro," Jack said. "Listen, Gigi, keep an eye on him while I'm gone. He looks like he fell out of an airplane, not down the side of the carriage house."

And with that Jack left the room.

"You really broke up with him?" Ethan asked.

"Yeah." I took a seat at the edge of his bed.

"Look, Gigi, if I ruined your chance to be happy, I'm sorry."

"That's not what you said before," I reminded him.

"I just didn't want you to get hurt . . . and instead I did just the opposite."

"It's not because of you, Ethan. You were right. It wouldn't have worked between me and Jack. I finally realized I don't love him," I said softly. "I loved what I thought he was—the most handsome, most charming guy in the world. Listen, thanks to you I learned that Jack isn't the kind of guy I want to be with. I want someone who's going to dance with me, not show off to his friends. Someone who's going to talk to me for hours, not just watch TV. Someone who's going to feel deeply about me and about life, not just live on the surface."

"Do you know anyone like that?" he asked quietly.

I didn't know what to say. I wanted to scream, "You, you dummy!" but after what Ethan had said to me before I practically pushed him out my window, I was afraid to admit it. He'd pretty much said he wasn't interested in me—that he would have done the same thing for any girl his brother was dating. And besides, there was Lydia.

"No, Ethan," I lied as tears started to fill my eyes. "I don't. I don't know anyone like that."

# *Chapter Twelve*

"Come on, it'll be fun," Becky coaxed.

"I don't want to be a fifth wheel," I objected for the tenth time.

"I know you want to see this movie," Becky said.

She just wouldn't let up. "Okay, I'll come," I agreed.

"Great. We'll pick you up at seven-thirty."

After Becky hung up, I wondered what I was doing. It had been two weeks since I'd broken up with Jack. Now he and Karen were an item. Becky and Andrew were likewise hot and heavy. And I was once again without a date on Saturday night, so Becky had invited me to tag along on her date with Andrew.

I couldn't decide which was more humiliating—not having a date or going to the movies with your best friend and her boyfriend.

Becky and Andrew picked me up on time, and we drove to the multiplex. There was a pretty long line to buy tickets.

"I'll wait on this line," I told them. "You two can get on the ticket holders' line so we'll get good seats."

"Okay," Becky said, and she and Andrew walked off arm in arm.

"Mind if I cut in line?" a familiar masculine voice said in my ear.

"Ethan? Hi." I felt that same rush whenever I saw him. Whenever I thought about him.

"Are you here alone?" he asked.

"Yes—I mean no, I came with Becky and Andrew. How about you?" I looked around, expecting to see Lydia Joyner.

"Nope. How about if we sit together?"

Feeling somewhat dazed, I waited in silence with Ethan to buy tickets, then found Becky and Andrew and gave them theirs. Becky saw Ethan behind me and gave me a questioning look, but I just shook my head. The next thing I knew, Ethan and I were sitting in the back of the dark movie theater, and he had his arm around me. After the movie was over I couldn't have told anyone the plot. All I could remember was the feel of Ethan's lips on mine when he kissed me.

And kissed me again.

*     *     *

I drove home with Ethan. When we got to my house, Ethan shut off the engine and we sat together in silence for a moment.

Neither one of us wanted to get out. The taste of Ethan's kisses lingered on my lips, and I ached for more of the same. But first I needed some answers to some very important questions.

I took a deep breath.

"What happened with Lydia?" I asked. "Aren't you two going together?"

Ethan seemed genuinely stunned. "No," he said. "Why would you think that?"

"I know you took her to Espresso Pacifico a few weeks ago. I just assumed . . ."

"Lydia just wanted to talk to me about her on-again, off-again relationship with Jack. She thought maybe I could shed some light on what was wrong between them."

"So what did you tell her?"

"I told her that Jack just wasn't ready to commit to any kind of relationship."

"So it wasn't a date?"

"No. Of course not."

I smiled through a sheen of tears that threatened to drop onto my cheeks.

The next question was even tougher. "So . . . you still like me? Even after I almost blew it by lusting after Jack? Even after I practically pushed you off the roof?"

He took me in his arms for a long, wonderful,

mind-blowing kiss. "Does that answer your question?"

"But, Ethan, I don't understand. When you were in my room, you told me you didn't do what you did because you cared for me. You said you were just protecting me, like you'd protect any girl Jack was dating."

"I lied," Ethan said, looking ashamed. "I didn't want to tell you the truth, that I had fallen in love with you. I didn't want to pick you up on the rebound from Jack. I needed to give it time. To make sure you were really over him."

Suddenly I felt claustrophobic in the Jeep. Ethan sensed my mood and came around to open my door. He took my hand, and we strolled through the Chandlers' grounds.

After a few minutes, Ethan broke the silence. "Could you do me one favor?"

"What?"

"It's a pretty big one."

I shrugged. "Just tell me what it is."

"Change your name."

"To what?"

"Gerolyn."

"But Gerolyn's so boring."

"I never thought so. And neither did anyone else. It's not the name Gigi or your new earrings or clothes or hair that makes everyone go 'Wow!' when they see you now. The changes are great, don't get me wrong. But all that stuff isn't as im-

164

portant as what's inside. And inside you're Gerolyn Pelka. Besides, can you imagine a serious journalist with the name Gigi? It sounds like something you'd call a pet poodle."

I noticed we'd ended up on the pool terrace—the same spot where Jack had danced with me. I briskly wiped away the tears that had suddenly begun to fall.

"There must be something terribly wrong with me, Ethan. It's not right to turn off my feelings for one guy and immediately switch on feelings for another."

"Did you ever think that maybe you've always had some feelings for me deep inside?"

I turned around and looked at him.

"I know a way we can find out if you really have feelings for me," Ethan added playfully.

My eyes widened.

He held out his hand. I moved closer to him, and a moment later we were kissing.

Fireworks.

Stars.

Hunger that had nothing to do with eating.

And perfection. Pure perfection.

This was for real.

When Ethan finally let go of me, I looked up at him. I never wanted to look away again.

I never did get back to Paris that year.

Instead I went to the prom with Ethan. We

tripled with Jack and Theresa (his latest—some things never change) and Andrew and Becky. I danced almost every dance with Ethan. His strong arms wrapped around me, guiding me gently across the dance floor. I felt like a princess in my pale blue silk ball gown. And in his tux, Ethan looked like a prince.

The last dance was a slow one. Ethan and I were still dancing after the music ended.

"I wish we could stay like this forever," I said, snuggling closer.

"We will," Ethan whispered in my ear. "Forever and ever."

And I think he's right.

*Dear Véronique,*

*I got your postcard from Spain today. I can't believe you eloped. That's so romantic. What is it like in Spain? The Costa del Sol sounds beautiful. I hope someday I'll get to see it myself.*

*I'm glad you included your temporary address in Spain. I'd been writing to you in Paris, and when I got no response, I thought you'd given up on me.*

*I have some good news for you. I'm in love—and it's for real this time! Not with Jack, but with his brother, Ethan. Incroyable!*

*It's too long a story to explain in a let-*

ter. I'll tell it to you in person—when I see you in three months!

I'm spending Christmas with the Thibaults, and Ethan is coming with me! He's never been to Paris, and I want to show him the Eiffel Tower, and the Arc de Triomphe, and everything else I love in Paris. But most of all, I want to show him something wonderful . . . how much I love him.

A bientôt.

Love,
Gerolyn

*Do you ever wonder about falling in love? About members of the opposite sex? Do you need a little friendly advice but have no one to turn to? Well, that's where we come in . . . Jenny and Jake. Send us those questions you're dying to ask, and we'll give you the straight scoop on life and love in the nineties.*

## DEAR JAKE

**Q:** *I've been dating this guy for about a week now and he keeps saying that he loves me. He says he adores me and that he'll never leave me. I know he's hoping I'll tell him that I love him, too, but I don't think I do! How will I know if or when I fall in love? How will I know if I'm in love with him?*

**TD, Saint Louis, MO**

**A:** Whoa! It's definitely time to tell this guy to slow down. Did you know each other for a while before you started dating? If not, then it's hard to believe that this guy really *loves* you. He's definitely head over heels for you, but the term "love" is premature. You can't expect to know a person well enough in one week to fall in love. Infatuation is more like it. If this dude keeps pressuring you to say the big "L-word," be honest and let him know how you feel. Make sure he understands that though you may not *love* him—yet—you really care for him. Tell him how special he is to you and that just because you don't love him now, doesn't mean you won't someday.

I don't think anybody can tell you the hows, whats, or whens of falling in love. It's different for everyone.

When *I'm* in love, I can't stop missing the person every time she's not with me. I love the person because she makes me feel so good about myself. Trust me when I say you'll just *know* when love hits you.

**Q:** *Two years ago, I moved to Virginia and met Danny—the boy of my dreams. We went out for almost a year, then my family moved to Texas. I'm still in Texas, and Danny and I write and call all the time. Well, here's my problem . . . We still love each other very much, but my mom won't take us seriously. She says it's just because Danny was my first love. I totally disagree. It's more than that. We want so much to be together, but how can we? All I can think about is him and how far apart we are. I'm so mixed up. My grades in school are dropping, and I'm falling behind. Please help me!*

**KI, San Antonio, TX**

**A:** Long distance is tough, isn't it? I know you probably feel like there's a gigantic hole in your heart that you just can't fill. One way to look at it is that if your love for each other is true, the two of you will find a way to be together again in the future. It might take months, even years—think of it as a trial period for your love. No one ever said love was easy.

In the meantime, accept the fact that you won't be seeing Danny for a while and try not to dwell on your painful situation. Sounds impossible? Why don't you try to focus on other things to keep your mind off missing Danny? Work on getting your grades back up. You just might be able to distract yourself long enough from your aching heart and make the honor roll at the same time.

# DEAR JENNY

**Q:** *Help! I'm so lonely. There's this really cute guy in my class, but I'm too afraid to speak to him. At this rate, I don't think I'll ever get a boyfriend. I never have the guts to ask a guy out. I don't think guys like me, because I'm ugly. What should I do?*

*SW, Tuscaloosa, AL*

**A:** Get rid of that "ugly" attitude! Focus on the beautiful side of yourself, whether it's your warm smile or the way you care for other people. Believe it or not, if you see yourself as beautiful, other people will see it, too.

Now about that cute guy: How well do you know him, and do you like him because he really is a great person or because he's just another cute butt? Now's the time to find out! It'll definitely take guts, but smile and say, "Hi! How's it going?" whenever you run into him in school. If he acts mean or cold toward you, you'll know he's a jerk and not worth your time. Most likely, he'll at least say "Hi" back. Eventually you'll find it easier to talk to him, and maybe you'll get a chance to know him well enough to feel comfortable asking him out. And if he says no, then hey, at least you took a chance. Thing is, you'll never know unless you try.

**Q:** *You probably don't get a lot of mail from guys, but I need a female point of view. I'm wondering what girls look for in guys. I mean, how do you get a girl's attention? What's the first thing you should ask her? Do you want to come over to my house? Do you want to go to the movies? There's someone*

*I like, but sometimes I don't think she even knows I'm on this planet. We have school dances, but I can't dance, so I don't go. What are the chances of a girl asking a guy out?*

*SL, New York, NY*

A: Finally! Just when I think there are no more sensitive guys in the world, along comes a guy who cares what we girls think! In general, I'd say that a girl wants to be treated the same way that you would want to be treated. She wants someone to be nice to her, someone to listen to her when she talks, and someone who likes her for more than just her looks.

If you want to get her attention, try talking to her. Maybe there's something the two of you have in common, whether it be a love for basketball or a certain kind of music. Once you find out what she likes to do, asking her out should be easy. If she likes to go to the movies, you can suggest the two of you go see the latest flick at the Quad. One thing's for sure. If *you're* the one who is interested in her, you better not wait around for *her* to ask *you* out or else you'll never get anywhere!

*Do you have questions about love? Write to:*

Jenny Burgess or Jake Korman
c/o Daniel Weiss Associates
33 West 17th Street
New York, NY 10011

*Life* after *high school* gets even *Sweeter!*

Francine Pascal's

SWEET VALLEY

SVU

UNIVERSITY

*Life after high school gets even sweeter*

Jessica and Elizabeth are now freshmen at Sweet Valley University, where the motto is: Welcome to college — welcome to freedom!

**Don't miss any of the books in this fabulous new series.**

| | | |
|---|---|---|
| ♥ College Girls #1 | 0-553-56308-4 | $3.50/$4.50 Can. |
| ♥ Love, Lies and Jessica Wakefield #2 | 0-553-56306-8 | $3.50/$4.50 Can. |
| ♥ What Your Parents Don't Know #3 | 0-553-56307-6 | $3.50/$4.50 Can. |
| ♥ Anything for Love #4 | 0-553-56311-4 | $3.50/$4.50 Can. |
| ♥ A Married Woman #5 | 0-553-56309-2 | $3.50/$4.50 Can. |
| ♥ The Love of Her Life #6 | 0-553-56310-6 | $3.50/$4.50 Can. |